HOLD ON TO YOUR DREAMS

Following her father's financial ruin and the untimely deaths of both her parents, Emily's comfortable life in Society comes to an end. Her pride prevents her from letting the man she loves know that her feelings for him are unchanged, so she throws herself upon the mercies of her aunt — a malicious woman. Although forced to work as a servant, Emily's dreams linger on. Will she ever regain her position in Society and her lost love?

KAREN ABBOTT

HOLD ON TO YOUR DREAMS

Complete and Unabridged

LINFORD
Leicester

First published in Great Britain in 2010

First Linford Edition
published 2011

British Library CIP Data

Abbott, Karen.
Hold on to your dreams. - -
(Linford romance library)
1. Life change events- -Fiction. 2. Social status- -Fiction. 3. Orphans- -Family relationships- -Fiction. 4. Aunts- -Fiction. 5. Love stories. 6. Large type books.
I. Title II. Series
823.9′2–dc22

ISBN 978–1–44480–640–3

Published by
F. A. Thorpe (Publishing)
Anstey, Leicestershire

Set by Words & Graphics Ltd.
Anstey, Leicestershire
Printed and bound in Great Britain by
T. J. International Ltd., Padstow, Cornwall

This book is printed on acid-free paper

1

Placing on the counter a tray laden with ribbons of every shade of pink ever imagined, the haberdashery assistant said pertly, 'Here you are, miss. I hope you will find what you want among this selection!'

Her somewhat abrupt tone and action, and her tight-lipped expression, betrayed her thoughts that this dowdily-dressed customer need not be fawned upon — not when the Misses Wilsden's Ladies' Emporium, situated in a London street not far from St James's Park, had the cream of the ton as its clientele.

Emily Harcourt felt her cheeks redden at the girl's attitude and inwardly berated herself for allowing the imperious tones and offhand manner to affect her still. She ought to be used to it by now, she reproached herself — but it never grew any easier.

Tentatively she reached out to touch the array of ribbons, hoping that the young assistant wouldn't notice how red and chapped her bare hands were. The discernable sniff of disapproval told her otherwise. She frowned in concentration, just knowing that whichever shade she chose, Aunt Augusta would consider that she had made an error of judgement. The knowledge that the ribbons were to be an added accessory to her cousin Juliana's gown to be worn at her eighteenth birthday ball did not help her decision, either. In Emily's opinion, the bright shade of pink that Juliana had chosen was far too garish and did not suit her cousin's colouring. Her tentative murmurs of this opinion had been sharply denounced.

'What do *you* know of fashion?' Juliana had demanded. 'Have you seen your own reflection in the looking glass lately?'

Emily needed no looking glass to know that Juliana spoke the truth. Since her aunt provided her only with clothes from the servants' hall, she had little choice over what she wore. Nevertheless, her cheeks had flamed with mortification at the unkind jibe.

She sighed heavily, remembering the gowns she had worn before her papa had died leaving nothing but debts behind him. Those days were long gone, as was her dear mama, who had eventually succumbed to an inflammation of the lungs, leaving Emily destitute and beholden to her only known relative. Mrs Augusta Simmons had grudgingly taken her into her home in the supposed capacity of an unpaid companion to Juliana, some four years her junior. Augusta never allowed Emily forget that it was only her charity that kept her out of the workhouse — or worse.

Emily endeavoured to be grateful to her aunt, but as she was frequently set to work in the kitchen quarters and dressed in the poorest quality of clothes, it was not always easy to sustain her gratitude.

The assistant stood tapping her fingers impatiently on the countertop. 'How about this one?' she suggested irritably, placing a ribbon of the shade of damask against the swatch of silk in Emily's left hand.

As Emily considered the effect of the two shades together, the door from the street burst open, causing a row of tiny bells to jangle merrily. This was followed by an echoing peal of laughter as, with a flurry of cold air, three young ladies swirled into the emporium, blown in, it seemed, by the blustery January weather. A tall gentleman engaged himself in closing the door, thus silencing the jangling bells and restoring the decorum of the emporium.

'What a wind!' one of the young ladies exclaimed and they all laughed again as they smoothed down their skirts and made sure their bonnets were still in place. Not wanting to draw attention to herself, Emily was careful to allow them no more than a flicker of a glance. She could tell that they belonged to the haut ton of Society and, freshly aware of the shabbiness of her own clothes, she quietly sidled her way along the counter towards its far end, sliding the tray of ribbons with her until she was sheltered by a tall potted fern. She concentrated hard upon choosing the right shade of pink ribbon, trying not to listen to the excited chatter and exclamations of the new customers, who, it seemed, had heard that a stock of muslin had arrived direct from Paris that very week.

The deeper tones of their male escort penetrated Emily's mind and she froze. It couldn't be! Not here! Not in so public a place! Oh, fate was too cruel! Of all the shops, why had they chosen this one? Even as the dreadful suspicion was taking root, it was confirmed by one of the young ladies exclaiming, 'Oh, Camilla! You must take note of what your brother says! After all, Mr

Brentwood's opinions are so highly thought of!'

Emily felt as though her heart had stopped. It was *him . . . them!* What if they recognised her? She would be so ashamed! She must leave directly.

She looked up, intending to whisper her excuses to the assistant but realised that the girl was glancing across the room, to where the owner of the emporium was displaying some bolts of lace to a customer of evident means. Emily followed her glance and saw the elder Miss Wilsden gesturing to the girl to leave her and to go to attend to the new customers.

The assistant shrugged and hissed, 'I know, Miss Wilsden, but this customer cannot make her mind up!'

'Leave her!' Miss Wilsden mouthed, flicking her hand peremptorily.

Emily's humiliation at being dismissed as of so little worth increased her agitation. She feared that the little altercation might have drawn the group's attention and her cheeks flamed as she sought to retain some dignity. 'I'm sorry!' she whispered, in tones barely audible. 'I will leave my decision for now and come back another day!' She turned to depart, still hoping to make her escape unrecognised. 'Oh!'

As she had agitatedly swung around towards the door, her reticule, which was dangling from her wrist, had caught around the edge of the tray and brought it crashing to the floor at her feet. Emily dropped to her knees in a frantic effort to scoop up the scattered ribbons and still make her escape, but it was not to be.

Miss Wilsden's cry of, 'Oh, really!' had carried clearly across the room and had gained the full attention of the other customers. Emily knew that they had all swung around to see the cause of the exclamation. She bent her face even lower, hoping that the brim of her bonnet might yet conceal her identity, whilst at the same time praying that her features might have changed unrecognisably in the five years since she had last seen her former friend at Miss Marshall's Seminary for the Daughters of Gentlemen at Bristol — and, more importantly, Camilla's brother, Mr Ralph Brentwood.

Emily scrabbled the ribbons into an untidy bundle, intending to turn away from the new customers as she rose but the assistant unwittingly thwarted that intention by coming around to the front of the counter to stand between her and the casually interested group. Emily was forced to stand up straight with her face towards her former friend.

She heard a sharp gasp. 'Emily! Emily Harcourt! It is! Whatever . . . ?'

To Emily's dismay, she realised that Camilla had left her friends and her brother and was approaching hesitantly across the tiled floor of the emporium. 'It is you, Emily, isn't it?'

Emily tilted her head down as she thrust the tangle of ribbons into the shop assistant's extended hand.

'I'm sorry! I'm sorry!' she gabbled helplessly to the open-mouthed girl.

She hurried towards the door, shielding her profile by raising her right hand to her bonnet, as if clutching at it on a windy day. 'No, you are mistaken, miss! I don't know who you mean!' she mumbled incoherently and, with her face still averted, she rushed out into the street.

After a frantic glance to her right, the direction in which she ought to be going, she turned left and hurried away, thankful that she had enough of her senses remaining to enable her to avoid passing in front of the multi-paned bow-window of the emporium, regardless of the fact that her steps were now taking her further away from her aunt's house. On top of everything else, she would now be late back, and that would mean more trouble!

In the emporium, Camilla took a hesitant step forward, as if to follow the fleeing figure, her attractive face frowning in concerned anxiety. However, she thought better of the impulse and instead returned to her brother's side.

'Ralph, I'm sure that was Emily Harcourt! You must remember. She was my friend at Miss Marshall's Seminary.' She paused, taking in the closed expression upon her brother's face and she grimaced at her own ineptitude. Of course he remembered! But he probably did not wish to be reminded about the lovely young girl who had jilted him all those years ago.

Ralph raised his right eyebrow as he favoured his sister with an impassive glance. 'Was she, my dear? I'm sure I wouldn't know. Now, are you going to order a length of that exquisite muslin? Or are you going to relinquish that delight to Miss Tildsley or Miss Appleton?'

Camilla returned his glance with exasperation, knowing that Ralph would not allow her to penetrate into the privacy of his long-ago lost love. She reluctantly pushed the puzzling encounter to a corner of her mind to think about at a more appropriate time.

Ralph Brentwood stood behind the

trio, smiling indulgently at their girlish chatter. However, if Camilla had turned around to look him in the eye, she would have discerned that his facial expression did not reflect his inner thoughts. His slightly narrowed eyes were cold and unfocussed as he replayed the short encounter over and over in his mind. The young woman had been Emily Harcourt; of that he was certain. Though it was a wonder they had recognised her, for her appearance was much changed from how he remembered her from five years ago. Her former sparkling eyes were now bright with only alarm and embarrassment, and her painfully thin face showed none of its former glow.

As for her attire, it was evident that her circumstances were much changed. But, whereas he might have expected to feel some self-righteous satisfaction at her lowly state, especially considering the anguish she had caused him when she had flung his declarations of love back in his face, he realised, much to his surprise, that he felt charitably disposed towards her.

Not that he imagined that he still loved her! That would be too extreme. Such adoration as he had bestowed upon her was born of youth and innocence, long ago discarded for a more mature bestowing of regard and affection towards any females who temporarily tugged at the strings of his heart. No, love was out of the question! And yet . . .

Unable to quell his tumbling emotions, he turned to gaze over his shoulder at the door through which Miss Harcourt had vanished, a thumb and forefinger thoughtfully stroking his chin. What had happened to her?

Oh, he knew she had been devastated by her father's sudden death — by his own hand, some had gossiped — but when he called to offer his condolences, Emily had refused to receive him. His ensuing letters were returned unopened and she had subsequently answered neither his letters nor those sent by

Camilla. Her only communication was a short stilted note that had accompanied the return of the golden locket he had given her as the token of his love. He had hastened to her home, only to discover that Mrs Harcourt and her daughter no longer lived at that residence. They had left at short notice, and no-one seemed to know where they had gone.

To a young man of no more than twenty years, Emily's disregard for his avowed love had felt a callous betrayal. He had imagined all who knew him must be sniggering behind their hands at his discomfort, and he had immediately persuaded his father to buy him a commission in the army.

The four and a half years as an officer in the Hussars, where his many dangerous military exploits as a scout had brought him a rapid rise through the officer ranks and filled the aching hole in his heart, now slipped away and he felt strangely subdued, as well as curious. Just what had happened to bring Emily down to this level of obvious poverty?

'Ralph.' Camilla's voice interrupted his musings. 'You were miles away! We've finished here and are going on to Henderson's. Come along, ladies.'

Ralph hastened to hold open the door and, as Camilla passed in front of him, she paused and raised herself onto tiptoe to whisper in Ralph's ear, 'I've made enquiries about Emily. I'll tell you later.'

Ralph raised an eyebrow, his features carefully controlled in an effort to imply that it was no concern of his. But his sister knew him too well.

* * *

Emily hurried along back streets she had not traversed before, becoming increasingly aware of the gathering gloom of dusk falling earlier due to the heavy layer of cloud. The temperature was dropping by the minute and Emily could suddenly feel the biting cold wind penetrating through her inadequate garments.

Her sense of direction let her down a couple of times and it was with some relief that she eventually recognised that she was on Grosvenor Street, not far from the grandiose residence her aunt had recently rented for the Season. Relieved to have found her way home, she turned and scurried to the rear entrance, determined not to give her aunt further cause for anger by ringing the front bell. She would be in trouble enough today, without incurring her aunt's wrath by repeating that particular error!

The warmth from the kitchen range enveloped her as she hurried through the outer door, murmuring apologies as a cold draught followed her in. The downstairs servants were seated at the scrubbed table and Mrs Penfold, the cook, paused in the act of pouring tea into an assortment of cups.

'There you are!' she exclaimed in exasperated tones mingled with some relief. 'Where've you been until this hour? Madam's been ringing down for you every five minutes for the past hour or so!'

'I'm sorry. I got a little lost,' Emily excused herself, turning towards the door that led upstairs.

'Not like that!' the cook chided. 'Madam won't want you in her drawing room in your outer things. Take your cloak and bonnet off but look sharp.'

As Emily began to divest herself of her cloak, she looked longingly at the dwindling pile of toasted crumpets that sat on a plate in the middle of the table, gleaming with melting butter — though her face felt so frozen she wasn't sure her mouth would open wide enough to eat anything.

Mrs Penfold followed her glance and quickly cut a crumpet in half, thrusting a piece into Emily's hand. 'Here — but you'd best eat it as you go!'

'Thank you, Mrs Penfold. You are an angel!'

It had been so cold outside that, now

she was in a much warmer environment, Emily's fingers and toes began to tingle painfully and she knew her face was unnaturally bright. She would have loved to have time to rub her arm and legs with a rough towel and maybe to linger by the kitchen fire and sip a hot drink — but such luxury was out of the question.

Inelegantly pushing the piece of crumpet into her mouth, she hurried up the back stairs, her heart hammering. She paused outside the drawing room door, wiped some butter off her chin and then rubbed her hand down her skirt. Knowing she could do no more to make herself look acceptable, she took a deep breath, pushed back her shoulders and held her head high before knocking quietly on the door. Without waiting for a reply, she stepped into the elegant drawing room.

Her aunt and cousin were seated near a glowing fire, their faces sheltered from its glare by embroidered fire screens. A small table laden with a light repast of pastries stood between them and a neatly dressed maid was in the action of pouring tea into two china cups.

'Good afternoon, Aunt, Juliana,' Emily greeted them, moving gracefully forward. She suspected her aunt would prefer her to remain a few paces away in an attitude of servility or, at the very least, to drop into a curtsey as she approached but she refused to demean herself in such a manner.

Augusta looked at her with a flicker of repugnance marring her face. 'You are late, Emily! You have taken a whole afternoon on what should have been a simple errand. It is little wonder that you had to fling yourself upon my charity in order to survive.' She let her glance slide up and down over Emily's form, her upper lip curling with distaste. 'The hem of your skirt is wet and muddy . . . and your shoes are only fit for the back yard.' She waved her hand dismissively. 'Well, as you can see, you are too late to partake of tea with us.'

Emily felt her face flame. 'Very well, Aunt,' she murmured quietly, hoping she would be allowed to return to the kitchen where she might share the servants' repast.

'What about my ribbons?' Juliana demanded. 'She hasn't got my ribbons, Mama. Where are they? Have you lost them?'

Augusta's gaze sharpened, instantly aware of Emily's hesitation in replying.

'Well? What have you to say, girl?' she demanded.

'I am sorry. I did not choose any,' Emily replied, trying to keep a note of defiance out of her voice. 'There were so many shades that I could not decide which you would prefer.'

'She's done it on purpose, Mama!' Juliana wailed. 'She is determined to ruin my ball!'

'That was not the reason,' Emily denied, her brain working feverishly. 'I . . . I wondered if you would prefer the Misses Wilsden to send a selection here so that you can make your own choice? You have such a . . . *distinctive* sense of taste, Aunt.'

Augusta held up her lorgnette and regarded Emily's flushed face with narrowed eyes. After a few silent moments, she lowered it again, apparently unable to detect whether or not Emily was simply using flummery to excuse her own laxness. 'Hmph!' she eventually grunted. 'I suppose that is acceptable. Very well, you may return tomorrow after I have consulted our engagement diary. I expect we can find a short time when we are free of engagements.' She waved her hand in dismissal. 'You may go, but do not forget Juliana will need you in half an hour's time to dress her for dinner.'

Emily readily made her escape, her head light with relief that she hadn't sunk to acting subserviently. She was determined, at all cost, never to lose her self-respect.

2

Having escorted his sister and her two friends to Camilla's opulent home, Ralph Brentwood warmed himself by the fire in the drawing room whilst the ladies scurried upstairs, chattering excitedly about their purchases.

Resting an elbow on the high mantelpiece and staring at the dancing flames, he begrudged the fact that the encounter with Miss Harcourt had banished the comfortable sense of languorous bonhomie that had settled upon him since resigning his commission after the battle of Waterloo had finally brought about the defeat of Napoleon and his return to England as a civilian. Following a promise to his mother that he would consider the possibility of choosing a suitable bride in the near future in order to secure the continuation of his family line, he had intended to look over the current Season's many hopeful debutantes with that idea in mind.

With most of Society removed from town throughout the Little Season, he had already enjoyed a number of light-hearted dalliances, pleasing numerous mamas and hostesses by his willingness to make up the numbers at balls, assemblies and other entertainments, without settling his heart as yet on any aspiring young lady. But the afternoon's encounter had thrown a shadow over that enjoyment. A tight band of . . . something, he wasn't sure what, now seemed to be squeezing his sense of contentment out of him — and he did not like it!

Why should he feel any guilt over having taken pleasure in his recent dalliances? He had not been the one to destroy the hopes of the other! He had not thrown Miss Harcourt's avowed love back at her feet and trampled on it! He had been the one to suffer the sidelong looks and insincere murmurings of sympathy. He thought he had put it all behind him — but here it was again, rearing its ugly head. And he was not sure what to do about it.

His thoughts were reflected on his furrowed brow, but he was careful to relax his features when the door opened and Camilla approached him across the softly carpeted floor.

His sister came straight to the point.

'According to the elder Miss Wilsden, Emily seems to be connected with a Mrs Simmons, a recently acquired client — here for the Season, Miss Wilsden assumes — bringing out her only daughter, apparently.'

She paused, wondering if her brother's bland expression was a true indication of his feelings.

'Connected in what way?' Ralph asked, affecting a show of indifference by flicking imaginary specks of dust from his immaculate jacket.

'Miss Wilsden felt unable to be precise on that point. Some sort of companion or lady's maid was her supposition on the first meeting, but she has made a number of unaccompanied visits, as today; though whether or not this is on her own account, Miss Wilsden does not know.'

Ralph considered this information silently, his face expressionless. When Camilla did not add any further comment, he asked casually, 'What sort of person is this Mrs Simmons? Is she kindly disposed toward Miss Harcourt? Does she treat her well?'

Camilla wrinkled her nose as she considered her words. 'Miss Wilsden did not say much about the lady but I gathered from her tone of voice that the lady in question is 'new money'.'

'And thus not worthy of respect?' Ralph queried, his eyebrow rising in a sardonic fashion.

'Only in so far as reflecting Society's well-held view,' Camilla reasonably pointed out. 'It doesn't signify very much in reality, as you well know. Some of our friends are 'new money' also.'

'So, Miss Harcourt may have found an amenable position suitable for an impoverished gentlewoman, and thus in no need of further enquiries?'

Camilla studied her brother's face, biting her lower lip as she considered his words. Was he as indifferent as he was making out? She was not sure. He had been very badly hurt by her friend's actions five years ago. 'I don't know,' she eventually admitted, her shoulders drooping in her indecision. 'There was something amiss. She didn't seem . . . well, *happy*, did she?'

Ralph's face was sombre. 'No. She was embarrassed, certainly, and clearly did not want our interference.' He looked away and stared again into the dancing flames of the fire. Whatever he saw there seemed to make him decisive on the matter. He looked coolly towards his sister. 'Then I think we should respect her unspoken wishes, don't you?'

Camilla's inner thoughts did not agree. Emily had been her best friend — and, although that friendship had been extinguished by Emily's abrupt disappearance five years ago and her lack of communication since, Camilla felt a flicker of concern and, if she were honest, curiosity stirring within her.

'Maybe,' she murmured doubtfully.

Ralph looked at her sharply. 'I do not wish to hear any more of it, Camilla. Miss Harcourt made her decision five years ago. We must leave it at that!'

Camilla suspected he might be right, but a surge of stubbornness prevented her from saying so. Her ears detected the sound of voices and it was with some relief that she turned towards the door.

'Ah, Mary . . . and Dora, there you are. Just in time to help us decide what we are to do after dinner.'

'And I, unfortunately, must take my leave of you, ladies,' Ralph excused himself, making his bow. 'I have an engagement this evening.'

Camilla was not altogether sorry to see his departure. She knew Dora was hoping Ralph might take notice of her more than he was accustomed to doing but, in his present darkly reflective mood, it was probably better that he was free to choose a more masculine form of entertainment.

As for herself, she had plans to make.

* * *

The following day was no less wintry than its predecessor but Emily was happy to leave the physical warmth of the house and brave the external biting cold wind, rather than endure the equal coldness of atmosphere of Juliana's presence. Juliana had complained unceasingly from the moment she opened her eyes at half past eleven in the morning.

'Ugh! The water is too cold! . . . Ouch! You are pulling my stays in far too tightly, Emily! . . . Don't pull my hair like that! . . . Now, see what you have done! You have spilled my face powder, and it was a new box!'

Emily knew that it was Juliana's hand that had knocked the box of powder onto the floor, but it was pointless to say so. That would have brought another tirade down upon her. So she merely fetched a brush and dustpan and swept up the delicately perfumed powder.

No, the outside chill was supremely preferable to her cousin's spiteful wrath. Emily held the edges of her mantle closer together and bent her bonneted head against the wind as she hurried along the streets to the Misses Wilsden's emporium. She could not help feeling apprehensive as she neared the shop. What if Camilla had decided to return in order to challenge her denial of knowing her? Or, worse, if Mr Brentwood were there instead!

It was with great relief that Emily saw that her fears were unfounded and she was able to deliver her aunt's request for a personal visit, setting a time for late the following morning. She chided herself for her unnecessary fears. Her own behaviour in cutting herself off from her friend had severed any responsibility Camilla might have felt towards her.

If Camilla had indeed given a moment's thought to her, it must surely have been only to despise her — and that was the due consequence of her cowardice. Even now, five years since she had deliberately cut herself off from the Brentwoods, she could not imagine having been able to follow any other course of action. Her family had been shamed — first by the loss of their entire fortune, and secondly by her father's suicide. It had shattered her dream of living happily ever after as Ralph Brentwood's wife.

Oh, Papa! Why, oh, why did you do it? We could have borne the shame of poverty. We could have started our lives again somewhere else. People need not have known. Together, we could have pulled through!

But with the added shame of her father's death by his own hand, her mother had simply given up and pined away. Her reason for living had gone.

But why could you not have lived for me, Mama? Emily's heart cried. *Was there nothing of worth within me to make you try for my sake?*

Emily knew there must not have been; otherwise her mother would have striven to recover. No wonder Aunt Augusta and Juliana treated her the way they did. It was all she deserved.

Her aunt's house was astir with a buzz of excitement when Emily returned to its confines. Cook was basking in the delighted aftermath of having served afternoon tea to 'Quality' and was generous with the leftovers of her baking. Emily had time to cram a couple of tiny cakes into her mouth and hurriedly drink a cup of tea before she was summoned upstairs to collect the tea trolley from the drawing room.

Augusta was in a rare benevolent mood. She beamed at Emily and raised her plump arms shoulder high.

'Oh, the honour of it! This will send Juliana's Season off to a fine start! There will be no limit to the benefits!'

She clasped her hands to her ample breast, her eyes shining. She turned to her daughter. 'What a hit you will be, my dearest! Such benevolence! Such condescension! Oh, I am quite overcome! Put another cushion behind me, Emily, dear! Ah, that's better!'

Fanning her flushed face, she leaned back against the cushions, her wide-open eyes unfocussed as she dwelt inwardly on the caller who has caused such a transformation in her demeanour.

Emily was nonplussed. Her aunt had addressed her as 'dear'! The Quality caller must have been special indeed to have wrought such a transformation! She looked at Juliana. Her cousin's glowing face matched Augusta's in its almost mindless delight.

'Er, has something pleasant happened?' Emily ventured, glancing from her cousin to her aunt and back again.

'Pleasant? Pleasant? A meaningless word!' Augusta chided, still purring with delight. 'Tell her, Juliana, dear. Tell her just who has condescended to visit us in order to *personally accept* the invitation to Juliana's ball!'

'It was . . . ' Juliana began.

'. . . Lady Westlake!' Augusta continued, giving Juliana no time to do more than speak the first two words. 'Lady Westlake herself! Such an honour! She came in person because she suddenly realised that our invitation had been mislaid and she was anxious not to cause offence by her tardy acceptance. Oh, I hope our neighbours saw her carriage outside our door! No doubt they will be making their calls in order to prise the details out of me! Just wait until they hear! What envy there will be! Tell her, Juliana! Tell her what grace her ladyship has! Oh, the honour!'

She sank deeper into the cushions and, for an anxious moment, Emily wondered if her aunt was about to have a seizure due to her excessive joy. However the moment passed and Emily felt able to turn her attention to Juliana, whose round, flushed face was beaming idiotically at her mother.

'So, who is Lady Westlake, Juliana?' Emily asked, sitting down beside her cousin. 'Is she a lady of note? One with great influence in Society?'

'Don't you know anything, Emily?' Juliana scorned. 'Lady Westlake is one of the most fashionable ladies in London. The very highest of the ton, if you must know! Of course, she wasn't *born* in the aristocracy,' she allowed, her voice showing a measure of censure. 'But her family are extremely plump in the pocket. She is married to Lord Westlake and she is reputed to have hosted the most lavish and delightful balls last Season. The biggest names in Society attended her functions.' Her eyes became dreamy and she clasped her hands at her bosom. 'Even the Prince Regent himself has been known to put in an appearance . . . and the most eligible of men, as well! Just think, Mama, we are bound to be invited back in return!'

'And she came here?' Emily asked, unable to disguise her incredulity.

'You needn't sound so surprised!' Juliana said peevishly, momentarily jolted out of her reverie. 'She has obviously made enquiries and decided to make our acquaintance. It will be an open door into the highest circles and I intend to make the most of it! Why, with Lady Westlake's patronage, I am more or less made already!'

'Yes, you probably are.' Emily smiled in bemused acknowledgement that her words were probably true, though she could not imagine why a Lady of High Society had desired the acquaintance of her aunt and cousin. Yet from the transports of delight that she was witnessing, there was no denying that it had happened. She fervently hoped her aunt and cousin knew how to deport themselves in such exalted company. The prospect of their subsequent humiliation if they did not made her quail within.

'Of course, when I heard that the Westlakes were in town so early in the Season, I just had to invite them, especially as they have a number of friends staying with them — and her brother, a hero from the Peninsular War, you know,' Augusta added, glancing indulgently towards her daughter. 'It will give Juliana such a start over the other debutantes if she can captivate an eligible party before the Season has even started! You will be the envy of all, my dear!' She paused and placed a finger coquettishly against her shining cheek. 'I wonder if I should send fliers to our lesser-known guests? No, maybe not. The surprise on their faces will be all the more gratifying!'

'I shall need more gowns and everything!' Juliana declared, rising from the sofa and twirling around the room. 'You must send for the modiste again, Mama! And maybe a hairstylist? Emily always does my hair the same way. It's so boring! And slippers, too! I shall need pairs and pairs of them! I don't want to look provincial in any way!'

'No, of course not, my dear. You will

look ravishing, I promise you. No expense will be spared!' Augusta assured her dotingly. Her beam faded as she glanced at Emily. 'And you must brighten yourself up a bit, too, Emily. You always look so pinched and dowdy. I know! We must make over some of Juliana's outmoded gowns. That will brighten you up somewhat.'

Emily suppressed a shudder as she thought of the bright silks and satins that Augusta favoured. 'I — I really prefer more gentle colours, Aunt Augusta. Maybe a cream or aqua gown would be nice?'

'Certainly not!' Augusta responded sharply. 'They would show wear far too quickly! Besides, such delicate colours aren't suitable for your position! Something more serviceable will do for you.' She reached over and playfully tapped Emily's knee. 'But you shan't disgrace us. Have no fear. I rather think your puce and emerald striped one might do, Juliana. I was only thinking it is becoming a little too tight for you.

Whereas you are so skinny, Emily, it will suit you splendidly.'

Emily's inner vision recoiled at the thought. 'There is no need, Aunt Agatha. No-one ever notices how I look, since you never let me stay in the drawing room when you have visitors,' she pointed out. 'I won't be seen.'

'I am thinking of when you attend Juliana at the routs and balls that she will be invited to!' Augusta pointed out as if to a simpleton. 'You will be there behind her on all occasions. Of course you will be seen!'

'No! I cannot be!' Emily protested in horror. She couldn't demean herself by appearing in such public places as Juliana's chaperone. Any number of people might remember her — not forgetting Camilla and Ralph! She had escaped from them once, but she might not be so fortunate another time.

'Oh, but you will!' Augusta countered. 'I can't have people thinking we cannot afford enough servants that I have to attend every function with

Juliana! Besides, you have had some experience of mixing with the upper crust. You will be able to help Juliana make her mark on Society. Why do you think I brought you here to London with us? I would have left you behind in Bristol if I thought you were going to be awkward like this!'

Juliana glared at Emily. 'She wants to spoil it for me, that's what! She wants me to look like an impoverished nobody! She's jealous of me!'

'No, indeed I am not,' Emily protested. 'I merely do not wish to be held up to ridicule in a public place.'

'Ridicule? Ridicule?' Augusta snapped, her voice high. 'I'll tell you what is ridicule! It is your ingratitude! If you know what is good for you, you will do as I say and attend Juliana at her ball or else I shall wash my hands of you! And I doubt anyone else would take in a useless, penniless chit like you! The choice is yours!'

* * *

The booming voice of the hired major-domo sounded over the music being played by the small orchestra, competing with the hubbub of conversations that filled the ballroom as guests took drinks and canapes from the hired liveried footmen and then gathered in small groups around the brightly-lit room.

Sheltering in the cover of some potted palms and ferns that broke the rectangular shape of the room, Emily could see the curled ostrich feathers that adorned Augusta's turban ducking and diving as her aunt, resplendent in a purple satin gown, received the guests with much bobbing and bowing.

Emily shifted her gaze to her cousin, miserably reflecting how she had failed to dissuade Juliana from wearing the low-cut fuchsia pink satin gown, richly adorned with ribbons and frills. Her hair was coiled on top of her head and her side ringlets were fastened with yet more of the bright ribbons purchased from the Misses Wilsden's emporium.

Emily took no comfort in the spectacle of the over-ostentatious garb of her aunt and cousin. Rather, she cowered even more at the shame she felt at being clothed in the most unbecoming gown she had ever had the misfortune to wear — far worse that her drab daywear. The only mitigating factor was that few of the guests gave her more than a cursory glance.

'Lord and Lady Westlake!' boomed the major-domo, bringing a spreading hush over the assembled guests.

Emily's wry acknowledgment that the 'surprise' factor far outweighed them having had foreknowledge of the illustrious guests was abruptly supplanted by horror as her curious gaze settled upon the beautiful face of the young Lady Westlake who was gliding forward on her husband's arm. It was none other than her friend, Camilla Brentwood.

Emily's attention was still transfixed upon Camilla when her subconscious mind deciphered the next introduction and she dragged her gaze to the small group of gentlemen and ladies who now filled the entrance.

'Mr Ralph Brentwood. Mr Philip Wraxley. Miss Appleton and Miss Tildsley.'

3

Emily's horrified gaze froze upon the group of new entrants to the ballroom. She found it difficult to take in that her friend was married, and was now Lady Westlake. That Camilla's status might have changed in their years apart simply had not occurred to her. Why should it? She had deliberately kept herself in ignorance of the lifestyle that had been denied her when her father died. Coping with her own change of status had taken full-time commitment.

She realised that Camilla's gaze was now slowly sweeping the ballroom and she drew back into the cover of the potted palm and ferns, her heart racing now that the immobilising sense of shock had diminished and her need of flight spurted adrenalin into her bloodstream.

But flight was impossible. There were

no doors in the part of the room where she sheltered. She would have to work her way carefully around the perimeter of the ballroom and hope that any door she encountered would lead to a place of concealment. She would face her aunt's wrath over her disappearance later.

As the Westlake party moved forward, other guests made way for them, bowing or curtseying. The Westlakes and their company graciously mirrored the gestures as they progressed slowly forward and pockets of excited conversations resumed in their wake.

Emily could feel panic sweeping through her. They were coming closer. If she did not move now, it would be too late. Keeping her face averted, she backed up against the wall and began to sidle towards the nearest door, skirting around any clusters of guests. She had lost track of where Camilla and Mr Brentwood might be and had almost reached the door when it was opened abruptly from the other side, impeding her progress.

'Oh!' She stepped back, colliding with someone behind her.

'Forgive me!' she whispered in apology. 'Oh!'

Ralph saw her face blanch when she realised with whom she had collided. Maybe he had been wrong to follow her, but his heart had been stirred by her scurrying to evade both him and his sister. He had hoped that Camilla might have pursued her former friend as she fled, but his sister has been engrossed in a conversation with Miss Appleton. Having no wish to draw a third party's attention to Miss Harcourt's flight, he had impulsively set off to intercept her before she vanished once again.

He had wanted to assure her that she need have no fear of him . . . that he would not hold the past against her.

'Emily . . . Miss Harcourt . . . '

To his consternation, he saw a red flush flow up her neck and spread over her face. She glanced wildly from side to side, but found no hope of escape from what was obviously a great embarrassment to her. He feared that he had made a great mistake in following her. He reached out a hand with the intention of gently assuring her that he meant her no harm but she backed away from him.

'Don't! Do not touch me!' A sense of panic was in her voice. 'I . . . er . . . I must get back to my aunt! She may need . . . '

Ralph was puzzled. 'Your aunt?' he echoed. 'You are here with your aunt?' He swiftly realised to whom she was referring and felt a sense of relief pervade him. 'Oh — Mrs Simmons is your aunt?' Then he had no need to feel concerned about her. 'So all is well, then. You are being cared for.'

Emily's face looked blankly at him, as if his words did not make sense.

'You are being cared for, are you not?' he queried, now with some doubt. 'Your aunt is kind to you?'

A strange expression flitted across Emily's face. An expression of — was it derision? Before he had decided, she tossed her head high and snapped, 'Obviously!' as if daring him to change his mind.

Ralph hesitated. This was not proceeding as planned. He had meant to reassure her that he held no resentment towards her; that the hurts had long since melted away. Instead, he was causing her distress. He glanced about them. Sets were being formed for the first dance and they were in danger of becoming conspicuous in their disharmony with each other. He must say his piece and get it over with; then they would be free to part.

'I wished you to know that I . . . was not irretrievably hurt by your sudden ending of our . . . friendship. I bear you no grudge over what happened. You must feel free to resume your friendship with Camilla. That is, if that is what you would like to do. It will cause me no discomfort to see you with her.'

Good heavens! He was gabbling like a callow youth. Why had Camilla insisted they attend? She must have known Miss Harcourt would be here! He was making a fool of himself. Just wait until he found his sister alone!

Emily was the one to bring their conversation to a close.

'Do excuse me, Mr Brentwood,' she hissed in brittle tones. 'You are making a spectacle of us!' She turned to go, but Ralph stepped after her and seized her arm.

'You are all right, are you not?' he asked with some concern in his voice. 'You look . . . '

'What?' Emily challenged him, abandoning her flight to face him again. 'Poor? A sight? A rag-bag?' Her throat had tightened so much that it almost hurt her to speak.

'N . . . no. That is . . . ' He paused and looked at her, this time taking in her outmoded, ungainly attire and pathetically thin figure. 'You look . . . unwell.'

'How gallant of you to say so!' she responded coldly. 'I will remove my pitiful self from your presence.'

She turned away again, only to be prevented from escaping once more.

'I will escort you back to your aunt.'

'Like a naughty schoolgirl?'

'Indeed, no.' His own cheeks felt as though they were burning. What had he done? How tactless of him! 'I am sorry. Would you prefer to dance?'

'No.' Her voice was barely audible.

'But you used to love dancing.'

'I am not dressed for dancing.'

He looked. No, he supposed she was not. In fact, now he came to look closely, she was dressed most strangely. He couldn't believe how he hadn't noticed before. He realised that the longer he detained her, the worse he was making her predicament. He straightened his back and then made a curt bow. 'I am sorry. I have placed you in an invidious position. It was not my intention. Slip away quickly before anyone notices us.'

Emily choked back a sob as she turned and fled through the nearby doorway into a dim passage. How dare he? He had the effrontery to stop her flight — and then, after everyone had witnessed her humiliation, he had the impertinence to order her to flee in case anyone had noticed his impudence!

She suddenly realised she was lost in a maze of passages. She wished she did not have to return to the ballroom, but knew she must, in case her aunt had not yet noticed her absence. Now that the dancing had started, she would require her to be in close attendance to Juliana.

She paused and took a few deep breaths, calming the sobs that seemed to be attempting to erupt from her throat. Thankfully, the threatening tears had not fallen. Anger at Ralph Brentwood's insensitivity had kept them at bay. What sort of gentleman was he, to feel free to assure her that her betrayal of him was of no account? To state that the resumption of her friendship with Camilla would cause him no discomfort? Could he not see that her status was now far inferior to his own, and even further beneath that of his sister? Did it not matter to him that they had once held tender feelings for each other? Obviously not!

She clenched her fists. She was determined not to let the incident cause her further conflict with her aunt. Her situation was precarious enough, without putting it under further pressure. If only there were some other means of her making a living! She would do anything — within reason — but her education and the few years since, when she had cared for her ailing mother, had fitted her for nothing other than being an unpaid companion. A life of misery, unless one were extremely fortunate; a life of servitude.

Her inner fury had restored her equilibrium. She looked around her and back the way she had come. Surely, if she turned right at the end of the passageway, and then right again, if that were possible, another door would give her access to the ballroom on the opposite side of the room from where she had departed?

With that intent, she hurried forward. Fortune smiled upon her. As she made the first turn into a more brightly lit corridor, she saw that she was passing an anteroom, from where the liveried footmen were emerging with trays of glasses of sparkling wine. She swerved aside.

'Refreshments for Mrs Simmons, please,' she requested. 'I will take it!'

She took the proffered tray from the footman's hands and swung away.

Back in the ballroom, the first dance was just coming to an end. Her aunt was seated in the place she had selected, her face set as her narrowed eyes scanned the room. Emily quickly skirted around the edge of the ballroom whilst there was still space to move there. She gave her aunt no time to ask where she had been.

'Here you are, Aunt Augusta! A refreshing glass of sparkling wine!' Emily lowered the tray. 'You must be parched after all those introductions!'

'What? Oh, it's you, Emily! I wondered where you were.' She took a glass and sipped the wine. 'Very nice; very nice. I said it would be just as good as the more expensive type. Now, no more gallivanting, Emily. I want you to remain here by my chair in case Juliana needs assistance in any way.' She threw up her hands in delight. 'Did you see Lord and Lady Westlake arrive? What a stir they caused! And the elegance of their friends! I have hopes in that direction, of course!' she added coyly. 'Oh!' Augusta hastily tapped Emily's arm with her folded fan. 'Don't look now; but they are glancing this way,' she hissed. 'I do believe they mean to come over! Get behind my chair, girl! You're blocking their way.'

To Emily's dismay, Lord and Lady Westlake were indeed approaching. Emily felt mortified. How could Camilla do this to her? The encounter in the haberdashery shop had been bad enough, but this was infinitely worse!

Was Camilla paying her back for her denial of knowing her? Had she no compassion?

Emily did not dare look at the approaching pair. She wished for the floor to open and swallow her. What sort of greeting would Camilla expect? A low curtsey? But that acknowledgement from a servant would be presumptuous! Any sort of greeting would be! Or did Lady Westlake intend to 'cut' her? That would be the most bearable. At least only she would know of it. Aunt Augusta would be oblivious to it; she was more likely to be astounded if Camilla greeted her.

Miserably, she stared at her hands clasped in front of her, suspecting that her cheeks were unattractively blotched with red patches.

'Lady Westlake! You honour me with your condescension!' Augusta gushed, rising from her chair and dropping into a wobbling curtsey. 'Please be seated, milady? Bring a chair for Lady Westlake, girl!' She waved an agitated hand towards Emily. 'Come on! Quickly! Quickly!'

Emily, startled, turned quickly towards a nearby chair but as she drew it forward she realised Camilla was smilingly dismissing her need for it.

'No, no, Mrs Simmons. I have not come to divert you away from your other guests. Though I must of necessity inconvenience you. I have torn the hem of my gown! Just look!' She swirled the hem of her skirt forward and then back again. 'It is so vexatious!' She gave a musical laugh. 'And I can't remember my way to the Powder Room. Do you think your maid could escort me? If it's not too much trouble?'

'Trouble? It's no trouble at all, milady! Come here, Emily! What are you doing, girl? Didn't you hear her Ladyship? Don't stand there looking like an imbecile! Escort her ladyship to the Powder Room immediately. Go on!'

Emily flushed at her aunt's imperious tone. With a swift flicker of a glance towards Camilla, she murmured ungraciously, 'This way, milady,' and, without checking that Camilla was with her, she set off towards the main doorway into the ballroom.

'Do slow down, Emily!' Camilla bade her in quiet tones once they were out of the ballroom. 'I need to speak to you, but I can hardly keep pace with you! I have no wish to trip over and draw attention to us!'

'But you do not mind drawing attention to *me!*' Emily hissed back bitterly. 'My aunt will be most displeased if word gets back to her that I used to know you!'

She noticed that Camilla winced at the past tense of the verb and was sorry if it caused her hurt — but did Camilla not see that their past relationship had no place in their present situations?

'Then let us find a quiet room where we can talk,' Camilla suggested. She glanced around and signalled to a footman. 'Is there an ante-room where my maid might attend to me?'

'Certainly, milady. Over here.'

He indicated a door across the way and led the way towards it, opening the door and holding it whilst they passed through. 'You will be undisturbed in here, milady.'

'Thank you.'

As the footman retreated and closed the door after himself, Camilla held out both hands towards Emily. 'Emily, my dear! After all these years! I despaired of ever seeing you again. Where have you been? What happened to you? How is it that you are so . . . ?' Her voice faltered to a stop. She was discomfited by Emily's refusal to take her outstretched hands and the lack of warmth in her expression.

'So come down in the world?' Emily suggested, her tone sounding more bitter than she had intended. 'Surely you must remember my father's business failure and his subsequent death? How did you think I would be after that? I wrote to tell you that it meant that I had to leave the seminary.'

'But it need not have ended our friendship, Emily. I wanted to help you! Ralph did, also. He was devastated when you sent his locket back.'

'But not for long,' Emily demurred wryly, remembering his words earlier. 'He assured me only this evening that he soon got over my rejection of him. Besides, there was no other course of action open to me. We were disgraced in the eyes of society, and penniless — we were unacceptable on both counts. My mother could not bear Society's open censure. We had to go far away where nobody knew us. It was the only way she could cope.'

'But, Emily! We were your friends! We wanted to help! Truly!'

Emily recognised the honesty in Camilla's voice and wished it could have been possible for her to have responded to her offers of help five years ago — but it was just as impossible now as it was then. Just as her mother's pride had barred her from accepting help, now her own pride prevented her laying her soul bare. There was little enough dignity in her life; her only tenuous hold on it was to hide the shame she felt.

She unconsciously straightened her spine and held her chin high. 'My mother and I had each other. It was all we needed.'

Camilla astutely picked up on the past tense. 'Had?'

Emily's shoulders sagged a little, but her chin remained elevated. 'She died last autumn. After that, my aunt . . . took me in.' There was no way she could tell Camilla of the humiliation of throwing herself on her aunt's compassion, of begging for help; pleading, even, driven by desperation; nor of the mortification she suffered daily. 'I am adequately cared for,' she added defensively.

Camilla's eyebrows rose. 'Adequately cared for? My kitchen maids are better turned out!'

Emily's face flamed with shame and Camilla immediately reached out to take her hands. Emily stepped away, putting her hands behind her.

'I am sorry!' Camilla apologised, withdrawing a pace. 'That was insensitive of me. Oh, Emily! Can you not see? I wish only to help you!' She spread her hands. 'I have ample means! It would count as nothing to me!'

'Nothing to you — but degrading for me!'

Emily knew she was deliberately twisting the meaning of Camilla's words, but she dared not soften her resolution not to accept charity, however well-intentioned that charity was offered. At least, with her aunt, she more than earned her keep, although Augusta frequently challenged that view.

However she regretted causing the emotional pain she saw reflected in Camilla's eyes and she forced a softening tone into her voice. 'I truly thank you for your concern. It means a great deal to me, but I implore you to believe that all is well with me. We cannot step back into the past. Even if you were not a titled Lady, my present status would be incompatible with yours, Camilla.' She bit her lower lip. 'I should not address you by your name but it has slipped out. Forget about me, please!'

Her impassioned plea hung between them in the silence that followed. Emily was afraid her resolution would falter if this conversation continued.

Camilla sighed deeply. 'Very well, Emily,' she reluctantly conceded. 'You are as sensible as ever. Go and fetch my maid from wherever she is. At least, then, you need not be untruthful to your aunt.'

Emily had turned to go when Camilla spoke again. 'However, if your situation deteriorates, Emily, do remember that I am still your friend.'

Emily wordlessly nodded and quietly left the room. But there was no joy in her heart as she thankfully made her escape.

4

The hour was late when Emily fell asleep that night. Although Juliana's party had been well attended, it had not fulfilled Augusta's aspirations of furthering Juliana's entry into the higher levels of Society.

'I wonder that Lady Westlake's brother and his friend bothered to come to Juliana's ball!' Augusta grumbled discontentedly as their carriage bowled along on their homeward journey. The carriage lamp cast an eerie glow into the confined space and Emily could see her aunt's lip curl in derision. 'No doubt, with his sister now a Lady, he probably has his eye amongst the nobility himself! Too proud for the likes of us, I dare say!'

'Maybe they realised that Juliana's card was full?' Emily suggested, trying to defuse her aunt's displeasure. 'Both gentlemen danced with the ladies of their party and a few other guests as well.'

'And what do you know about that?' Juliana demanded. 'Were you staring at them? Do you not know a maid should stand with her eyes cast down? No wonder you never noticed when I needed your attention!'

'But they didn't dance with Juliana! Neither of them! Not a single dance!' Augusta indignantly asserted, paying no heed to her daughter's complaint. 'Surely they knew Juliana would scratch out other names if they requested a dance! Would you not, my love? Why do they suppose they were invited?'

'To swell the numbers?' Emily murmured, staring at the darkened window of the carriage, but seeing only the pale reflection of her own face. 'To enhance your guest list by their presence? Did you not say what an honour it was when Lady Westlake accepted the invitation?'

'Pshaw! It was no use them coming if

they didn't intend to dance with Juliana!' Augusta scorned. 'Everyone will be laughing at us! Delighting in poor Juliana's humiliation! She may as well have been a wallflower as not to be asked to dance by the Quality! But you showed them, my poor dear, didn't you! You didn't sit out a single dance!'

'It was probably the look on Emily's face that put them off!' Juliana sneered petulantly. 'Every time I was brought back to your side, Mama, she looked as miserable as a wet week in January! Were you jealous, Emily? Did you wish you were dancing? You said you used to like dancing. Did you wish some young buck would ask you? It happens in novels, you know! A handsome rake asks a serving wench to dance — usually on the balcony or in a back corridor. Is that what you were doing when I saw you slip out of the ballroom just before the dancing began? I bet she was, Mama!'

'Don't be silly, Juliana. No one would ask Emily to dance. Not unless he were half-blind, at any rate!' She snapped her glance back to Emily. 'So, get that hoity-toity look off your face, girl. There'll be trouble if I learn that you deterred any of Juliana's potential suitors from requesting a dance with her. And it's no use scowling at me like that! If this is what a night out mixing with Society does to you, there won't be any more of it! Maybe it wasn't such a good idea to take you on as Juliana's maid after all. I should have known you would try to spoil it for her!'

'I did not,' Emily protested wearily. She wished she had danced with Ralph Brentwood! It would have sent her aunt apoplectic, but at least she would have done something to merit this censure.

'But I need a maid, Mama!' Juliana wailed. 'Every debutante has a maid! Only you said we couldn't afford a proper one.'

'Hmm!' Augusta demurred, her eyes narrowed as she considered her niece. Emily returned the look impassively. She would prefer not to be Juliana's maid. There was no joy in it. Only potential embarrassment at every social engagement.

'Ah! I know the very thing!' Augusta declared, beaming at Juliana. 'I shall take Flossie out of the kitchen and give her a try. She will be so grateful, she'll do it for no extra money! And take that smug look off your face, my girl. You won't be sitting around with idle hands. You will take over Flossie's work, starting as soon as you have assisted Juliana to prepare for bed!'

* * *

Ralph Brentwood spent a restless night. It had not been a successful evening on any count. After leaving the Simmons girl's insufferable ball, he had gladly accompanied Jack Westlake and Philip Wraxley to their Gentlemen's Club at 37 St James' Street. He found he had no great desire for gambling and his half-hearted presence at the card table was more of a distraction to his fellow gamblers than any benefit. When his party left White's in the early hours of the morning, the effect of the cold air made him realise that he had imbibed far too much alcohol in the effort to deaden his mind to the memories of five years previously.

In response to his brother-in-law's suggestion that they hire a cab, Ralph had eased his shoulders into his many-caped coat that an obliging footman was holding out for him and shook his head, grimacing at the unpleasant pounding within his skull caused by the movement of this small action.

'I'll walk,' he slurred briefly, wincing as his voice echoed within his head.

He eventually let himself into his London house, thankful that he had given his footman and butler the evening off, and unsteadily made his way up the stairs to his bedroom suite.

'Good evening, sir!' his valet murmured, as he opened the door and stood aside to allow Ralph to pass.

Hopkins silently removed Ralph's coat and jacket and pulled his boots off his feet. 'Will that be all, sir?'

It was a rhetorical question. Any answer at all would have surprised him. With the clothing draped over one arm and the boots in the hand of the other, the servant quietly backed out of the room, knowing his master would be more ready for conversation sometime after noon the following day.

His complacency was shattered when he heard his master moving around after no more than six hours in bed. Hurriedly dragging on his clothes, he made as calm an entrance to the room as he could manage under the circumstances.

'Good morning, sir! A bright day it is, too!' he said cheerfully, crossing the room to draw back the curtains. 'You are dressed!' he exclaimed reproachfully as he turned around. 'You should have called me, sir.'

'No matter.' Ralph dismissed his concern. 'I have decided to go out early.

No, do not disturb Mrs Bagley. I shall find a bite of something in the kitchen on my way out.' Seeing his valet's woebegone expression, and knowing that Hopkins would have a long face all day if he thought his master was out and about without his ministrations, he added, 'You may help me on with my boots and jacket, since I have already disturbed you.'

Ralph was glad to be out of the house. He needed some fresh air and hearty exercise. If his head were in a better state, a few rounds with Gentleman Jackson might have been just the thing. As it was, a brisk gallop in Hyde Park was the only alternative he could think of — and the earlier the better, if he was to escape the censure of Polite Society, who frowned upon anything faster than a leisurely canter within the boundaries of the Park.

The stable lads managed to conceal their surprise when he made his early appearance, and his favourite stallion was saddled in a few minutes. With a brief salute of his riding crop, Ralph left the confines of the stable yard and made his way to Hyde Park, his sedate pace belying the turmoil within. The truth was, his conscience was uneasy. He had no clear idea of what he had said amiss in his conversation with Emil — Miss Harcourt, he realised he must accustom himself to calling her — but he knew that something had increased the anguish in her eyes during their inadequate conversation at the ball.

He had meant to put her at her ease; to convince her that friendship with his sister was not out of the question, especially not in relation to himself and their former friendship; that he had put their liaison aside, the hurts forgotten — except that the latter was not strictly true, was it?

Oh, he had thought it was. His years on the battlefields had dulled the ache and blunted his sense of loss when his attempts to console Miss Harcourt had been denied with a curtly written note. But seeing her again had allowed the wound and disappointment to resurface and had strengthened his resolve never to let a woman hurt or reject him again. Was that why he had spoken carelessly at some point? Had his inner pain surfaced in his words without him being aware of it?

He was no nearer to solving the problem when he arrived at Hyde Park and, after making sure there was no one in the near vicinity, he cantered to the open grassland in the centre of the three hundred and fifty acres of lawns and groves and gave his horse his head. Jupiter did not disappoint.

The ride was exhilarating and made him long for the meadows and open countryside of his country seat, regretting his decision at the start of the year that he ought to make some effort to look over the young ladies on the current marriage mart.

He had felt none of his present turmoil when exchanging pleasantries with either Miss Tildsley or Miss Appleton, his sister's house-guests, and he knew, from their blushes and winsome glances through quivering eyelashes, that his attentions were not unwelcome. Maybe he should simply return home, spend what was left of the morning in a leisurely fashion and then repair around to the Westlakes' house in Mayfair and see if some light-hearted dalliance might help him choose between the two equally suitable prospective brides?

On the other hand, was the Simmons' residence not just a little further away on the slightly less fashionable side of Grosvenor Street? Surely, it would be better to seek an audience with Miss Harcourt, put right any wrong he had unintentionally inflicted upon her the previous evening and make an end to the matter?

Thus resolved, he left Hyde Park and turned in his chosen direction, impatient now to carry out his plan and then be free to let his life fall into the easy pattern he had imagined it would take on resigning his commission. He was not betraying Miss Harcourt. She was the one who had made the decision to end their friendship; he was merely finalising that decision.

The sedate pace for horse-riding along the fashionable street calmed the turbulence within his breast rather more than he wished, and his doubts resurfaced as to the wisdom of his arriving on horseback at what he feared was an unfashionable time for making calls. However it would surely be excused, since it was customary to pay a courtesy visit to compliment a hostess on an enjoyable evening's entertainment. Not that it *had* been enjoyable, but he hoped that was irrelevant. He would have to pretend it had been, as a prelude for asking if he might speak with Mrs Simmons' niece.

He dismounted, tied the horse's reins to the railings and nimbly ran up the steps, resolutely ringing the bell before he gave way to his misgivings. He frowned. The sounds of some sort of disturbance seemed to be going on beyond the closed door. He once more considered departing, but he had taken no more than one backward step from the door when it opened and he was confronted by a red-faced footman.

Beyond the footman, Ralph could see the young lady whom he recognised as the daughter of the house. She was shrieking abuse at a maid and pulling her hair, her face contorted with anger. The maid, whom Ralph was relieved to see was not Miss Harcourt, was matching the girl scream for scream. Further back again, the portly figure of Mrs Simmons appeared, screaming, 'Get back to the kitchen, girl!'

'Ouch! It weren't me! She knocked it out of my hands!' the maid protested, her hands trying to restrain her mistress from tugging at her hair. Crunching under the feet of the two young women, Ralph could see the shattered remains of what had been a loaded tea tray, now spread across the hallway floor.

His presence had not yet been noticed by anyone other than the footman. He fished in his pocket for his card. 'Ralph Brentwood,' he introduced himself, handing it to the footman. 'Maybe I should call at another time?'

His diplomacy was wasted. Maybe it was the low sound of his voice that stood out against the bedlam around him, or the movement of his arm as he offered his card. Whichever, the mayhem in the hall ceased abruptly as all faces turned in his direction.

Miss Simmons' fingers released the girl's hair, her lower jaw having dropped inelegantly open. Her mother's face was undergoing a range of expressions from anger, dismay and embarrassment to a parody of beaming welcome that resembled an exaggerated grimace.

'Mr Brentwood!' Mrs Simmons exclaimed, staggering forwards across the broken crockery and squashed pastries, her hands outstretched towards him. 'Oh, whatever must you think of us? Such a to-do!' She attempted a light-hearted laugh. 'One just cannot get decent servants these days! They have no idea how to behave in an upper-class home. Well, get down and pick it up, girl! Can you not see we have a visitor? You, man! Don't stand gawping! Go and get a brush or something! Anything!'

For an insane moment, Ralph wondered if she were referring to him. His startled expression penetrated Mrs Simmons' outrage and she flapped her hands towards him. 'Not you, Mr Brentwood! Not you! Do come in, sir!' She gestured wildly towards the doorway that framed her daughter. 'Stand aside, Juliana! Let Mr Brentwood step inside! And smile, girl!' she hissed in an undertone as she manoeuvred Juliana into the room in front of her.

Ralph remained where he stood. He had no wish to step into the drawing room and engage in superficial conversation with this dreadful woman whilst her abused servants cleared up the remains of the light repast.

'I will not intrude, ma'am,' he said curtly. 'I came merely to — er — thank you for your hospitality last evening and to request if I might have a few words with your niece, Miss Harcourt. But, it is obviously an inconvenient moment and I shall — '

Mrs Simmons stared at him, her expression aghast. 'With Emily? You wish to have words with Emily? What on earth for?'

Ralph mentally kicked himself. He had not intended to make his request so bluntly. No wonder Mrs Simmons was outraged. A visitor, especially a male visitor, did not ask to speak with a maid, and that is what Miss Harcourt's position seemed to be within this household. However, his own outrage was rising and his control was in danger of slipping. He drew himself up tall and glared coldly at the woman in front of him.

'Miss Harcourt was — is — a friend of my sister. They were at school together. My sister is, naturally, concerned to see her so diminished in life. We wish to ascertain that all is well with her,' he finished weakly. It was obvious no-one could be well in this household!

'Of course all is well with her!' Mrs Simmons screeched. 'What has the ungrateful wretch said to you?' She turned to draw the still shocked, scarlet-faced Juliana to her bosom. 'My dear girl said she had seen her talking to you, didn't you, dear? How dare she disgrace us like this? After all the charity we have bestowed upon her!'

Ralph made a curt bow.

'Madam, I have no wish to continue this conversation. Send someone to bring Miss Harcourt here immediately and we will be on our way.'

'You can't take her with you! I won't allow it! I know enough about Society to know that such an action will cause a scandal!' Mrs Simmons' bosom heaved in indignation. 'Get out of here! Go on, get out, before I call a servant to throw you out!'

'You can't take her!' Juliana burst out defiantly. 'She's gone! And we don't know where!'

Ralph was momentarily deflated. He did not blame Emily for leaving her aunt's household. It was a wonder she had stayed so long! But where would she be? How long was it since she left? She could be anywhere in London. He did not know what he would do if he found her but, somehow, he felt responsible for worsening her plight.

'Then I will find her,' he said quietly. 'Do you know where she may have gone?'

Mrs Simmons's eyes narrowed. 'No, I do not,' she declared haughtily.

Ralph was not sure he believed her, but could hardly say so. He made another curt bow, now wishing only to get out of the place. 'Good day, ma'am. Miss Simmons.'

He turned and strode towards the door. The footman, who had resumed an impassive posture, hastened to open the door. He stood erect, his eyes staring blandly ahead.

'Miss Harcourt is in the kitchen,' he said quietly, hardly moving his lips.

Ralph halted. 'Is she, indeed?'

He turned abruptly and strode down the hall to the rear of the house, past the flustered Mrs Simmons and her gawping daughter.

'Where are you going!' Mrs. Simmons demanded. 'You have no right — ! How dare you, sir?'

Ralph raised his eyebrow. 'Oh, I dare, ma'am.'

5

Ralph let his instinct guide him to where the kitchen might be. When he flung open the door at the top of a flight of steps, he saw three anxious, upturned faces gazing at him in some trepidation.

The older woman must be the cook, he reckoned; the maid he had already seen; and the third was the strained, pale face of Miss Harcourt. His heart contracted at the anxiety portrayed there.

'Ralph?' He heard her gasp his name as he stepped forward.

Against all rational thinking, he longed to run down the steps, snatch her into his arms and carry her from this dreadful house, but Mrs Simmons' words had reminded him that such an action could only lead to scandal. Instead, he paused, smiled benignly and calmly descended the steps.

'Miss Harcourt, I have come to convey you to my sister's home,' he said in measured tones, as if they had earlier made such an arrangement. 'Are you ready?'

'Oh!' Emily was nonplussed. She was not sure exactly what had been happening upstairs and Flossie's hysterical account of it had not been particularly enlightening, but, if the shouting and screaming that had drifted along the corridor was any indication, something untoward had occurred.

'Don't you dare go with him!' Augusta screeched, now framed in the doorway recently vacated by Ralph Brentwood. 'If you do, you will not be welcome back here! I'll not have my charity flung in my face like this!'

'You go with the young gentleman, Miss Harcourt,' Mrs Penfold quietly muttered. 'You deserve better than this.'

Emily was bewildered. She had refused Camilla's offer of employment the previous evening. How could she now run to her? She unconsciously wrung her hands together as she stared at Ralph. What should she do?

Ralph's facial expression was still of bland enquiry but the glint in his eyes told her that he would brook no arguing.

'Y . . . yes, I am ready,' she stammered. 'I will just go and fetch . . . '

'You will take nothing from this house, you ungrateful girl!' Augusta shouted, beginning to stumble her way down the steps.

Ralph took hold of Emily's arm and turned her towards a door he had spied in the corner of the kitchen. His hope that it led to the outside was well-founded. He would have preferred to leave by the front entrance, but had no desire to submit Miss Harcourt to a close encounter with her aunt.

Their imminent departure increased Augusta's venom. 'I'll see you ruined!' she bawled, adding, 'Both of you!' as if to dispel any other interpretation of her threat. 'Society will scorn you! You will never be accepted! I shall see to it!'

Ralph turned to confront the red-faced woman staggering towards them. He looked down upon her from his greater height, his upper lip curling slightly as he spoke.

'I think, ma'am, that Society will be more incensed by your mistreatment of your niece,' he said coldly.

Augusta teetered to a standstill, his calm assertion halting her progress as no wild threat would have done. 'Mistreatment?' she echoed, one hand fumbling backwards for the end of the stair rail and the other fluttering at the base of her neck. 'I hope you are not implying that I . . . '

Ralph raised one eyebrow and regarded her with a steely stare. 'I imply nothing, ma'am. I state a fact.'

'Ohh!'

The shock of his words seemed to cause a wave of giddiness to sweep over Augusta. Ralph took advantage of her brief halt and firmly guided Emily outside into a small cobbled yard that contained a number of outbuildings and had a brick wall around its boundary. His arm closed around her waist as he propelled her forward.

'This way,' Emily directed, an overpowering sense of unreality possessing her. She turned towards a wooden gate that led into a narrow back entry; they hurried towards it, anxious to end this degrading episode.

'Come back! Come back! We need to discuss this!' Augusta cried, her voice breaking into wails of despair as she realised that Emily and Mr Brentwood were ignoring her pleas.

The sounds of her frenzied cries faded as they hurried along the narrow entry. Emily felt numb. Her legs were almost giving way beneath her and, without Ralph's arm around her waist, she knew she would crumple to the ground. They turned right, heading towards the main street. As they reached the street, Emily stumbled and almost fell headlong. Only Ralph's hold on her prevented the tumble. He held her close as he looked urgently along the street to where he had tethered his horse.

'Damn!'

The word was breathed, rather than spoken. It was only now that he recalled that he had ridden to the house, and not driven in his carriage. Although few people had been astir when he had enjoyed the gallop in the park, a number of pedestrians and carriages were now nearby. None near enough, as yet, to require a greeting — some but would soon be near enough to notice that Miss Harcourt was in some distress.

He could not place her on his horse. Even if the saddle were suitable, it would not do. Jupiter needed a firm hand, and Miss Harcourt was in no condition to provide it. How the devil . . . ?

'Ah!' His breath eased out of his lungs as he recognised the approaching carriage and the horses that drew it. His dilemma was solved!

He swept Emily into his arms and hurried forward. The coachman's expression did not flicker as he drew up alongside his mistress's brother. Camilla was already at the window of the carriage and reaching a gloved hand to open the door.

'Ralph! What on earth . . . ?'

'Step back!' Ralph commanded, as the door swung open. 'Let me place Miss Harcourt inside!'

Camilla drew back, staring at her brother in amazement as he placed Emily tenderly onto the front-facing seat. 'I was about to make a call on Mrs Simmons, but I see you have beaten me to it! Oh, Emily, my dear!' Camilla seated herself beside her friend and drew her into her arms. 'Whatever has happened? No matter! Come, lean against me.'

'Take her home with you, Camilla,' Ralph said, stepping back. 'I'll come along later and explain what happened.'

As the coach began to move, Emily

collapsed against Camilla. The self-control she had managed to summon during the confrontation in the kitchen now left her and she quietly began to sob. Someone who cared for her was in control of her immediate future. Beyond that, she could not contemplate.

* * *

When they arrived in Grosvenor Square, Camilla lowered the window and spoke to the coachman.

'Drive round the back, Gates.' She turned to Emily, murmuring, 'It will be more discreet that way. The fewer people who see your arrival, the better.'

Emily was grateful. She did not mind that Camilla was ashamed of her presence. She would stay only a short while until she felt recovered from the ordeal. Maybe a hot drink in the kitchen. But where would she go then? The enormity of what she had done, what Ralph had persuaded — no, commanded — her to do hit her. She was homeless! She had nowhere to go; nowhere to live; no means of earning a living.

'Oh, Camilla, what will become of me? I have no one to turn to!' she cried in despair.

'Nonsense, Emily! You have me and Ralph. We will take care of you. Do not worry; you are in safe hands. Now, I wish you to remain here for a few moments whilst I speak with Mrs Gates, our housekeeper. She will prepare a room for you and we will convey you up there as soon as we can. Are you able to walk, do you think? It will be much easier if you can.'

'You . . . you mean I can stay the night?' Emily queried. 'Are you sure? I do not wish to cause you any embarrassment.'

Camilla laughed. 'Silly goose! Of course you are staying the night! And longer. You are not to worry. Wait here.'

It was slightly more than ten minutes before she returned, though it seemed far longer to Emily. Her head was spinning and she wished she could lie down somewhere and simply be allowed to sleep. Last night, after insisting that she helped Juliana prepare for bed, her aunt had sent her down to the kitchen since she was no longer Juliana's maid, and she had had no option but to curl up on a chair in front of the kitchen range and sleep there. It was still dark when she was wakened by Cook's arrival in the kitchen and she had grimly described her demotion to kitchen maid and Flossie's elevation to lady's maid.

Flossie protestations that she 'didn't know nothin' about being a lady's maid' were swept aside by Augusta's mid-morning arrival into the kitchen. After denouncing Emily as an incompetent hussy, Augusta waved a dismissive hand in her direction. 'Put her to work, Cook! I suggest scrubbing the kitchen floor and all the downstairs passages for a start. I will come back to inspect her work before luncheon. Tomorrow she can do likewise at the front of the house. Make sure you have the task finished before any decent people are abroad, my girl!' she added sharply, malice shining in her eyes.

Gloating at how she was bringing her ungrateful niece down to size, she then hustled the over-awed Flossie upstairs to tell her her duties.

Emily was not totally ignorant about the lot of a kitchen-maid, for had she not acted as such whilst her dear mama was still alive? However, it was one thing to tackle the many household chores for the comfort of herself and her mother, and quite another to satisfy the demands of a vindictive woman whose aim was to demoralise her.

Emily was determined not to do so. She already regretted turning down Camilla's offer of help last night. She must now beg her forgiveness and ask if she were still prepared to help her. She must know a great many people. Surely someone was in need of a maid of genteel upbringing?

She leaned her head back, trying to detach herself from her tumbling thoughts. Too much had happened too quickly and she was so tired.

'Come, Emily, dear.' Camilla's voice roused her. 'Hold onto my arm and take your time. Mrs Gates has organised everyone to be busy elsewhere, so you need not fear anyone seeing you in your present state.'

Emily felt the faint remnants of her pride curl in distress but she understood the reason for Camilla's caution. Her friend was now a titled lady. She would not want anyone to know that she was inviting a person of no means into her home. Servants talked, so the less they saw or knew, the less there was for them to gossip about. She must become immune to such unintended slights causing distress.

With her head down and shoulders hunched, Emily accompanied Camilla into the house and up the back stairs to the upper floors and was disconcerted when Camilla opened a door that revealed a plush carpeted floor beyond.

'In here, Emily,' Camilla urged.

The room was so light and beautiful it took Emily's breath away. The walls were predominantly cream with damask pink and gold trim. The full-length curtains and the cover on the bed were damask rose. The cupboards and wardrobes were painted cream, as was the soft carpet into which her feet seemed to have sunk up to her ankles.

Emily shrank back. 'N . . . no. You cannot mean . . . It's much too grand. Look at me. I am dressed in tatters.'

'I will soon rectify that, Emily. First, my maid will bathe you and I will find some gowns for you. Now, come. Mrs Gates cannot keep everyone busy elsewhere for long; I do not wish anyone to see you as you are at present!'

Emily's resistance seeped away. Camilla was right. She was unsure how Camilla was going to explain her presence, but fewer untruths would need to be told if no one saw the state of her as she arrived.

A hipbath was situated in front of the blazing coal fire. Although Emily had always washed herself down every day, it was so long since she had sunk into the luxury of a hot bath that she made no protest when Camilla began to unbutton the bodice of her gown.

'Now, you must not mind me helping you, Emily. I want you to be in the bath when Nancy sees you.' She picked up Emily's discarded gown and underclothes in her fingertips and held them at arm's length. 'I hope you have no attachment to these garments, for I am going to take them straight to the kitchen and tell Mrs Gates to burn them! Your aunt must be a monster to make you wear such degrading clothes!'

She picked up a large bath sheet and held it in front of her, giving Emily some degree of privacy. 'Now, step into the bath and relax. Just let me unpin your hair and pour a jug of water over it. There!' She suddenly giggled. 'It just goes to show that, without our clothes, we are all the same! No one will now dare to suggest you are anything other than a genteel lady!'

* * *

Less than an hour later, Emily, dressed in a lacy silk nightgown, her hair arranged into a high knot of becoming curls, was reclining against a pile of soft feather pillows with a tray of nourishing broth and delicious fresh bread rolls upon her lap.

Camilla was seated at the end of the bed, her hands clasped around her knees and her toes tucked under the edge of her skirt, just as if they were still at Miss Marshall's Seminary and about to share girlhood secrets.

'You still look exhausted, Emily,' she said with concern. 'But Mrs Gates will soon have roses back in your cheeks and more flesh on your body.'

'Why are you being so good to me?' Emily asked. 'I do not deserve your goodness, especially after refusing your help last evening. I am sorry I turned down your offer of employment. It was pride.' She gave a bitter laugh. 'Even the poor have pride, you know.'

Camilla reached forward, touching her arm. 'I did not offer you work, Emily. You are here as my friend. Whatever happened five years ago has not changed that.'

Emily's face fell. 'But what will become of me if I do not get employment? I cannot impose on your friendship for ever. A few days, yes. I am grateful for this.' She swept her hand around the room. 'But once I am strong, I must move on.'

'We are friends, Emily,' Camilla said firmly. 'If our roles were reversed, you would do just as much for me, so let me hear no more of it. We will face the long-term future when the need arises!' Her tone softened as she continued. 'Now, when you have eaten, you must rest for a while. Have a sleep if you can. I plan to send our house guests out on a carriage drive that we had organised. I will tell them that I have heard from a dear friend from my school days who has been unwell and that I have invited you to stay whilst you recuperate. When they return, you will be dressed and in the drawing room, as if you have just arrived, and we will carry on from there.'

'What if they recognise me?' Emily said. 'They'll know I am acting a lie.'

'Do not concern yourself about that!' Camilla laughed. 'It is a common fact that many of the gentry would not even recognise their own servants if they met them away from their posts of duty, and they barely caught a glimpse of you either in the haberdashery shop or at your cousin's ball. As for your acting a lie, far from it! You *are* here as my dear friend, and that is the truth! In fact . . . ' Camilla paused, looking suddenly thoughtful.

'Yes?' Emily prompted.

'Well, I think your being here could be a real blessing in disguise, as it were,' Camilla said slowly. 'It is a rather special house party. You see, Ralph is undecided about which of my two friends he should consider asking to be his wife, so I have got this party together to help him to get to know them better. Their mamas are here as well, so it is all perfectly respectable. I expect you saw them at your cousin's ball.

'Of course, I have arranged a number of balls and outings with other young people, but your being here makes it less obvious. It will balance any rivalry between Mary and Dora, and make everyone much more relaxed.'

Emily was not sure. Camilla's two friends may look upon her as a rival for Ralph's affections, but she could soon put them at ease on that matter. Although her heart had felt a slight pang when Camilla said Ralph was thinking of asking one of her friends to be his wife, she had long ago dismissed her chance of becoming his wife. That dream had gone forever.

She sank back against the pillows.

With the hot broth inside her, she felt physically better already, and her friend's words had eased the worry about both her immediate future and her fear of being an intrusion into the house-party. Sleep was already stealing upon her when Camilla carefully climbed off the end of the bed, gently removed the tray and tiptoed from the room.

6

Dressed in a day gown of cornflower blue muslin, into which Camilla's maid had hastily sewn some tucks so that it would better fit Emily's slender figure, Emily was seated cosily by the fire in the drawing room listening to Camilla's account of how she had met and married the dashing Jack Somergill, the young Lord Westlake, when the other members of the house party returned from their outing.

Camilla had just described a humorous anecdote that had caused Emily to laugh with spontaneity. Her cheeks were the colour of fresh roses and a genuine sparkle brightened her eyes — eyes that exactly matched the colour of her gown — as both young women turned their heads towards the door. Two young ladies entered the room, one of them exclaiming, 'Oh, we had such fun, Camilla! You should have come with us!'

They were followed by a man Emily recognised as having seen at Juliana's ball, as well as Camilla's brother, Ralph. Camilla stood up and went to draw her friends forward towards the sofa where Emily was sitting.

'Come and meet my dear school friend, Miss Emily Harcourt. I was delighted when she agreed to join our house party. Emily, this is Miss Dora Tildsley and this is Miss Mary Appleton. We met last Season and vowed to renew our acquaintance this year as soon as we were back in town.'

Emily rose from her seat and all three ladies bobbed a small curtsey to each other. 'I am pleased to meet you,' Emily smiled, thankful that the lessons of deportment and etiquette that she and Camilla had been taught at Miss Marshall's Seminary in Bristol still remained within her. Although nervous, she managed to turn quite calmly towards the two gentlemen.

'You remember my brother, Ralph, of course,' Camilla continued, allowing time for Ralph to make his bow and Emily to respond, before adding, 'and his friend, Mr Philip Wraxley.'

Emily was glad that the introduction of the other gentleman had followed on so quickly after Ralph had bowed to her, as the sight of him had sent a surprising tremor through her body. Blushing becomingly, she turned and bobbed a curtsey towards Mr Wraxley, who remained by her side, obviously at ease in this drawing room.

'Are your mamas joining us?' Camilla asked her two friends.

'Later,' Miss Tildsley replied for both of them. 'They are to have a short rest and join us shortly before dinner.'

'Good. Now, come and sit down and tell us all about your carriage drive,' Camilla suggested, gesturing towards the group of easy chairs arranged near the fireplace. 'I am glad the sun kept shining for you. One can never be sure of the weather so early in springtime.'

'It was beautiful — and Mr Brentwood lived up to his reputation of being a nonpareil at the reins of his barouche!' Miss Tildsley breathed in husky tones, as she seated herself on the sofa, admiration shining from her eyes. 'I am convinced that any other driver would have had us overturned into a ditch, but not Mr Brentwood. Do sit here, Mr Brentwood, and tell me how you achieved such prowess!' She patted the seat beside her, smiling coyly and fluttering her eyelashes unashamedly at him.

Ralph obligingly tossed back the tails of his coat and sat at an angle on the designated seat, somehow managing to make his tall figure seem elegantly at ease.

Emily hardly dared look at him. The younger Ralph she had known would have been nauseated by such mawkish behaviour as Miss Tildsley had shown. However, on this occasion, he merely smiled faintly and murmured, 'Not at all, Miss Tildsley. There was nothing out of the ordinary in my handling of the reins. Mr Wraxley, here, has a much finer reputation than I.'

Emily glanced at Mr Wraxley, who had seated himself in a chair next to her, to see how he dealt with Ralph tossing the accolade into his court and wondered if he, too, were a foil in the plot to ease his friend's progress into the right choice of a bride.

'Some might dispute that,' he demurred calmly. 'Though I confess I am eager to see how my new greys perform at speed. I would not at all mind setting them against those prime bits of blood of yours, Ralph.'

Ralph cocked a questioning eyebrow towards his friend, as Miss Appleton clapped her hands together. 'Ooh, yes! A race! May we ladies join in?' She turned to Camilla, forming her lips into a girlish pout. 'I pleaded with Mr Brentwood to allow me to try my hand at the reins today, but I was unable to persuade him!'

'I am not surprised!' Camilla laughed.

'My brother, like most other young men, is very particular about whom he allows to handle his teams. I doubt he would even let me handle that specific pair, even though he knows I have a good hand.'

'And you did seem a trifle nervous, Mary, dear,' Miss Tildsley said in tones that seemed a little too sweet to be genuine, Emily thought.

Miss Appleton's pout changed into a more genuine one and she turned to face Miss Tildsley. 'Well, at least I didn't squeal with alarm quite as often as you did! Nor did I continually clutch at Mr Brentwood's arm on the return journey! If anyone might have landed any of us in a ditch, it was you, Dora!' She turned back to Ralph. 'I thought the return drive most exhilarating!'

Emily was quite disgusted to see Miss Appleton now fluttering her long lashes at Ralph and then casting her eyes down with a maidenly blush. She would be ashamed to employ such feminine wiles. If they thought such antics would endear them to Ralph, she was sure they were mistaken. Not that Ralph looked as appalled as he might. His glance between the two young women was quite indulgent. It occurred to her that Ralph had changed somewhat in the past few years. She peeped at him through her eyelashes as he conversed with easy charm, parrying the sniping comments the young women tossed towards each other.

He was no longer the young man she had instinctively known could not have coped with her sudden reversal of fortune five years before. He had matured. She supposed she had, too. Neither of them was the person they had been. With a flash of insight, she realised how harsh her actions had been in not allowing him to speak to her; not replying properly to his letters; not giving him the reason for breaking off their relationship.

But it was now in the past and there was nothing she could do to change it. She had forfeited her chance to hope for anything other than friendship with Camilla's brother — and he had now cast his hopes elsewhere.

A tiny frown furrowed her forehead. If Ralph were so undecided between Miss Tildsley and Miss Appleton, did that mean that, really, he was in love with neither of them? That was a pity. Although she knew that many Society marriages were not love matches, she still cared enough about him to want him to marry for love. A marriage without love must be very hard to bear.

Yes, she thought, *perhaps Camilla was right*. The way these two young ladies were behaving towards each other, maybe her presence here would balance things out. She would also be able to console the luckless Mr Wraxley, who, at the moment, seemed tolerantly amused to see his friend the object of such blatant adoration and competition for his attentions.

And it would be quite interesting to see how the Misses Tildsley and Appleton endeavoured to become the one chosen to be Ralph's bride — and which, if either, succeeded.

'And you, Miss Harcourt, have you been in town long? Is it your first visit?' Mr Wraxley spoke at her side.

Emily allowed her speculations to drift away as she turned to face Mr Wraxley. He seemed a pleasant young man, of average height, dark brown hair cut fashionably short and brushed forwards over his forehead.

'Yes, it is my first visit.' She smiled at him. 'And no, I have not been here long. I know Camilla has told you of my mother's death last year. I — I'm afraid I found life difficult for some while, but that is behind me now and, thanks to Camilla's kindness in inviting me here, I am looking forward to my visit to our capital city.'

'And you are quite alone in the world?' Miss Tildsley asked, an eyebrow upraised as if she found the notion to be somewhat demeaning.

'Er, yes,' Emily agreed, 'though I have an aunt and a cousin. But they — '

A third gentleman entered the drawing room, thankfully drawing their attention away from Emily, making further explanation unnecessary.

'Ah, there you are, Jack,' Camilla smiled. 'You are just in time, my dear. Mrs Gates will be sending up some refreshments any minute.'

Emily saw that Lord Westlake's glance went immediately to Camilla, and Camilla's expression softened in response. That was how it should be between husband and wife, Emily decided. A warmth of joy in each other's presence. How fortunate they were.

* * *

With just five other guests invited to dinner that evening, the occasion was, thankfully, semi-informal. Emily, seated between Mr Wraxley and another quietly-spoken young man named Mr Harding, was content to sit quietly and listen, responding to conversation on either side of her when necessary. After dinner, most of the young people went to the theatre, an engagement that Camilla felt duty-bound to keep.

Emily was thankful for the opportunity of an early night. By good fortune, fate had, in less than twenty-four hours, propelled her from a life of drudgery to life among the haut ton of Society — and she needed time to recover from the harshness of her recent regime.

Three more young ladies, their mamas and maids arrived the following day, coincidentally, to Emily's relief, taking the limelight away from her. She was no longer the unexpected newcomer exposed to probing questions. Jenny, her maid generously assigned to her by Camilla, was a recent addition to the Westlake staff and, as such, was readily absorbed into the hierarchy below the stairs of the well-run household.

As each day passed by, filled with a seemingly endless round of carriage drives, visits to museums, travelling fairs, a military review and a number of privately hosted parties, Emily was quickly integrated into the friendly group, with only casual questions asked about her presence amongst them. The easy manner between herself and their hostess placed her in a position beyond dispute.

At times, she wondered how many of the young ladies were there to be looked over by Ralph Brentwood, with a view to his being desirous of making an offer.

Each day, he brought a number of male friends to join in their outings and entertainments, all of whom, under the vigilant eyes of the mamas and other chaperones, obligingly escorted the ladies on the varied excursions. Emily could see individual preferences beginning to show — so much so that she feared if Ralph did not make a move to show his preference soon, he might be in danger of losing out to his more decisive friends. Miss Tildsley still managed to put herself at the forefront of most occasions but, although Ralph was unfailingly gallant in his dealings with the assertive young woman, as far as Emily could determine, he shared his gallantry equally to one and all — including her.

She knew this was an act of kindness, born out of his affection for his sister, and she schooled herself to react in the same manner; as indeed she did towards the other young men. She supposed that only Ralph knew about her total lack of fortune and therefore shied away from becoming too responsive to friendly overtures, since, if she encouraged any young man to reach a point of wishing to declare himself, she would have to straight away dispel any illusions he might have about her prospects. And, if that became public knowledge, her delightful experiencne of life among the more favoured of society would be well and truly and over.

Oh, she knew it would be over at the end of the Season. She could not expect Camilla to support her forever — but she was so enjoying the experience. The memory of it would remain with her throughout the remainder of her life and sustain her through whatever was in store for her when it was over — but not yet! Let it last a little longer!

'Are you happy, Emily?' a quiet male voice asked in her ear.

They were at a private ball in the magnificent town house of Lord and Lady Blanford, and Emily was temporarily without a partner. She had chosen to stand out for the current lively country dance and had positioned herself near the long curtains that draped an open a patio window. The gentle breeze of a fine spring evening drifted into the ballroom and she was revelling in its freshness.

She did not have to turn around to know it was Ralph who had spoken to her. In spite of her knowledge that her action of the past had separated them for ever, she could not rid herself of the special fondness she held for this man. He had matured from the charming but sometimes rather gauche young man he had been in his early twenties, and fulfilled all his early promise of becoming everything a woman would desire from the man of her dreams — but that was all it would ever be for her. A lost dream.

Nevertheless she felt no bitterness. She had his friendship; that would have to suffice!

She turned to face him. He was standing close behind her and she felt startled by his nearness. The fragrance of whatever male perfume he wore assailed her senses, making her feel deliciously light-headed. His lips were parted slightly, his expression smiling as he awaited her answer.

She remembered their stolen kisses of years ago, and could not help wondering what it would be like to be kissed by him now. Her lips parted and she unconsciously ran the moist tip of her tongue over them, setting them a-tingling, almost as if she had indeed been kissed.

'Ohh!' Her breath escaped almost silently and she felt her cheeks burn at her outrageous thoughts. She glanced around, hoping that no-one had noticed and, when she looked at Ralph again, the intensity of his expression caused her heart to flutter wildly. He seemed to be looking into the depth of her soul, his expression so caring that a tremor ran through her. She knew she was in danger of betraying her true feelings, and that must never happen. He would not dare come near her if he suspected she still cared for him, and she needed to see him! She needed to know that she could venture into his presence, even when he had chosen the woman he wished to marry. She would learn to live with that. But she could never live with the knowledge of his scorn.

She stepped away and forced herself to laugh lightly. 'Why, yes, I am happy, Ralph. You and Camilla have been so kind to me. I had lost all hope of being able to enjoy anything like this. I no longer even dreamed of it!'

'Ah, hold on to your dreams, Emily,' Ralph said softly. 'I have not lost mine. One day, I hope to — '

'Ah, there you are, Mr Brentwood!' A commanding voice interrupted him. The magnificently bejewelled figure of their hostess was descending upon them, her hand gesturing imperiously. 'The next set is being formed and I believe a young lady is awaiting you over there, Mr Brentwood. Miss Littler — in the pink satin,' she added helpfully, noticing his rather blank expression.

'Oh! Yes, of course!' He strove to regain his composure. 'Excuse me, Miss Harcourt.' He bowed briefly and departed in the direction indicated.

'Now, Miss Harcourt, is your card marked for this dance?' Lady Blanford enquired pleasantly. 'No? I hoped not. A late arrival to town this Season has just begged to be introduced to you and to solicit your hand for this dance. Come, my dear. Ah, here he is.'

She led Emily towards a tall,

elegantly dressed young man who had the fairest hair Emily had ever seen on a man. His blond curls fell in studied disarray around his handsome, slightly petulant face. His eyes, paler blue than her own, seemed to gleam with an intensity that Emily found unsettling.

The young man bowed his head slightly at her approach and looked towards Lady Blanford for the introduction.

'Miss Harcourt, allow me to introduce Mr Guy Maitland to you. Mr Maitland, Miss Harcourt.'

The greeting smile on Emily's face froze — and, for a fleeting instant, it seemed Mr Maitland was as startled as she. His recovery was swifter. He took her hand in his heavily jewelled one and made an elegant, if slightly extravagant, leg. Still holding her hand, he straightened up, his face now coolly impassive. 'Miss Harcourt,' he murmured.

Oblivious of the tension between them, Lady Blanford declared, 'There! Enjoy the dance! You are just in time. They are holding a place for you.'

Mr Maitland inclined his head slightly towards the dance floor and Emily felt obliged to step forward with him and take her place in the nearby set — but her mind was in turmoil, her memories tumbling back to the time of her father's disgrace and eventual death just over five years ago.

Her father's business partner, the man who had supposedly lost all of his wealth at the same time as her father, was called Walter Maitland. She did not recall there being a son, but it was not a common name — and she was sure that he also had appeared startled when he had heard her name.

But if his father had been equally ruined by the business failure, as he had claimed — and thus unable to throw out a lifeline to her father — his son showed no sign of it. His whole appearance declared him to be a man of wealth. How had he made such a dramatic recovery?

7

Emily knew not how she executed the movements of the dance. All she could think of was that her partner was, in all likelihood, the son of the man who had claimed himself as ruined by the failed shipping business as Tobias Harcourt had been; that he was unable to help to subsidise the business in the hope of an eventual recovery. Yet it seemed he had, somehow, managed to make good his losses.

Emily was thankful that the moves and figures of the dance gave little time for conversation between partners and, if Mr Maitland had attempted to talk to her, she later assumed she must have given suitable replies.

In spite of the fact that Mr Maitland had not commented, Emily felt certain her name meant something to him; but, when the dance ended and he offered his arm to lead her back to her place, he gave no sign of having the same troubled thoughts as her. His expression was, however, remote and, under normal circumstances, a young lady might have wondered what she had said to make her partner wish to part so coolly from her.

As it was, Emily was relieved that she was now free of his presence. Should she have asked him outright if he were indeed related to her father's final business partner? No, it was neither the place nor the occasion for such a direct question and she did not feel composed enough to be able to deal with the answer, had it been positive.

Oh, she wished she might find Camilla and ask to return home — but that would be spineless behaviour! No, she must somehow get through the remainder of the evening. She glanced at her dance card. The next two dances were claimed by young men who had joined the Westlakes' house party on most days, both amiable youths who would offer light flirtation, expecting only the same from her.

She controlled her agitation well and, as her mind settled, it occurred to her that Mr Maitland's appearance of wealth might be as flimsy as her own. Attired as she was in Camilla's passed-on gowns, she knew herself to be portraying an affluence she did not possess. Was Mr Maitland in similar circumstances? In which case, who was she to criticise his attempts to put the past behind him and look to his future?

Having almost managed to satisfy herself on that score, Emily felt the tension draining from her, and by the time the supper dance was announced she was feeling more relaxed. Mr Wraxley had written his name on her card for that dance. He came to claim her just as Ralph joined a nearby set with Miss Tildsley, and they were just in time to make up the same set. Ralph glanced at her with apparent concern and she wondered if he had seen her with Mr Maitland. Did he know of his connection with her father? Probably not, since their business had been centred in Bristol.

Miss Tildsley, she noticed, bore a rather smug expression and clung to Ralph with an air of possessiveness. Her heart felt suddenly heavy. Was Miss Tildsley the one whom Ralph favoured most? She hoped not. There would be no chance of continuing any sort of friendship if that lady became his wife. She pushed her concerns away and smiled at Ralph, not wanting him to suspect anything amiss. She must learn to stand on her own feet.

It was late when they arrived back in Grosvenor Square, and no one lingered in the reception rooms. Emily was thankful to submit herself to Jenny's ministrations as she prepared her for bed, but, tired though she was, it was a long time before she managed to fall asleep.

Her mind kept returning to Mr Maitland's position. Was he not as well-heeled as his attire suggested? And was he intent on hiding his lack of wealth in the hope of making a beneficial marriage? He would not be the first to do so; it would be the only recourse left open to herself, were she to choose marriage over obtaining employment as a means of providing for her future existence. Was he afraid she would spread malicious gossip about him? After all, he probably knew as little about her as she did about him.

Maybe she should reassure him that she had no such intention? It was their fathers who had been in business, not them. And, unless he was being deliberately devious in the matter, it was surely none of her business. It would be up to the father of any wealthy young woman to make his own enquiries about any supplicant for a daughter's hand in marriage.

The restless night, with a recurrence of dreams that had started after her father's suicide, left Emily feeling washed out. For once she was happy to linger in bed and break her fast in the quietness of her own room.

By the time she descended to join the more robust young ladies, Ralph and some of his friends were already there. Emily made a general greeting to those present and gradually wended her way towards a window embrasure that overlooked the street, where she could pretend to be absorbed in watching passers-by.

'Is something worrying you?' Ralph murmured quietly behind her. His expression was caring and she considered whether or not to confide in him.

'Camilla mentioned that she felt something had happened to take away your composure last evening, though she said she later wondered if she had imagined it,' he continued. 'I was sorry our conversation was interrupted when it was. Was it I who disturbed you? Was I speaking out of turn?'

'No, of course not,' Emily responded in surprise. She could not imagine to what he was referring. 'No, it is merely . . . ' She paused and glanced into the street, tempted to share her concern over Guy Maitland.

No, it was too complicated. Besides, her concerns were probably unfounded and she had no wish to pass further problems onto Camilla. Both Camilla and her brother had done enough for her already. She must not add this to their burden. She must, somehow, see to it herself.

What she needed was an opportunity to meet privately with Guy Maitland and put his mind at rest about any misgivings he might have about her intentions — which meant she had to be prepared to move away from the shelter of Camilla's household and into Society in general. And she may as well start this very night.

She turned, impulsively laying her hand on Ralph's arm. 'I so enjoyed the ball last night; it made me realise I have been too reticent about joining in the wider activities Camilla has planned for her guests. Would it be possible for me to change my mind and be in the theatre party this evening?'

Ralph looked surprised but made no effort to discourage her. 'Of course. We have two boxes reserved for us. You will be more than welcome.'

Emily's maid was delighted to dress her for such an outing. 'It's time you went out and about, miss,' she chattered. 'You'll enjoy it, I'm sure. Oh, you look beautiful, miss! You'll have all the gentlemen ogling you!'

Emily gazed at her reflection. She was dressed in a heavy silk gown of royal blue with layers of flounces around the hem. She wore a matching tightly-fitting spencer with long fitted sleeves that puffed out over her upper arms and a wide-brimmed beaver bonnet decorated with curled feathers.

They travelled in four carriages, each emblazoned with the Westlake coat of arms and driven by coachmen, since the gentlemen of their party would be accompanying the ladies inside. Drury Lane was crowded with carriages and others arriving on foot and the carriages had to wait in line as they edged closer to the dropping-off place by the ornate front entrance to the Theatre Royal. Emily was entranced by the elaborate décor of the foyer and could not resist turning herself slowly around so that she might take it all in. She was unaware that the others in her party had moved on in the crush and she felt a little alarmed when she realised she could see no one she recognised. She knew they were to watch the play from a box — but where was it? Had they gone up the stairs to the right or to the left?

She glanced from one flight of stairs to the other, trying to remain calm but finding herself flustered by the crowds milling around her.

'Surely that's Emily, Mama!' A piercing voice suddenly sounded above the general hubbub of the theatre-goers.

Emily turned to face the direction from which the voice had come, drawn by the sound of her own name. Her cousin Juliana stood a few feet away, her face red with indignation. A harsh laugh followed. Aunt Augusta was standing just behind her daughter, a malevolent gleam lighting up her eyes.

'Ha! Has the rake who abducted you from my house now left you to fend for your living as a Cyprian?' Augusta scorned loudly. 'How dare you flaunt yourself in decent Society!'

Emily felt her face flush. She did not know the exact meaning of the word Augusta had called her but her tone of voice conveyed its significance. She drew herself up. 'No, ma'am!' she said coldly. 'I have simply lost my party.'

'Ha! Lost your virtue, more likely!' Augusta railed, flicking her skirt away in an exaggerated gesture of contempt. 'Get back in the green rooms, girl, where your sort belongs!'

Emily flinched as a hand gripped her elbow. 'This way, Miss Harcourt. Allow me to escort you to your box.'

Emily twisted around and was amazed to see that her rescuer was Mr Maitland. He stood close beside her, shielding her from some of the stares of those around them.

'Th . . . thank you, sir!' she stammered, a sense of shame washing over her. He must have heard Aunt Augusta's words! What must he think? Her legs felt weak and she was thankful to cling to his arm for a moment.

'Ha! Got another one now, have you? Just like I said, you're nothing more than a trollop!' Augusta sneered. Her lips curled in derision. 'We had a lucky escape when we got rid of you! Come, Juliana! Let's get some fresh air!' And she dragged Juliana away.

'What a dreadful woman!' Mr Maitland said lightly. 'Do you know her?'

'She is my aunt,' Emily replied faintly. 'She is my only relative. I lived with her for a while.'

'How unfortunate! Well, I shan't hold it against you. No one can choose their relations. By the time you have them, it is generally too late to do anything about it! Now, whose party did you say you are with?'

'I didn't.' Emily smiled, suddenly light-headed with relief that the unpleasant incident was over. 'I am with Lord and Lady Westlake. They have a couple of boxes somewhere but it is my first time here and I am afraid I do not know where they are.'

'I do. If you will be so kind as to take my arm, I will escort you to them.'

With a slight bow and a bemused smile, Mr Maitland held out the crook of his arm and Emily thankfully laid her hand upon it, smiling up at him. Her heart felt full of gratitude towards him. Why did she allow herself to spend the whole of last night in turmoil about him?

'I was hoping I would meet you again,' she confessed candidly. 'I feel we have things to discuss; to sort out, regarding our fathers' business affairs.' She felt his arm stiffen and paused to look up at him. 'You are Walter Maitland's son, are you not?'

'Well, yes. I — '

'Emily! There you are!' The exclamation drew her gaze to the top of the flight of stairs that they were about to ascend. Ralph was hurrying down the steps, his face concerned. The two men bowed stiffly to each other and Emily released Mr Maitland's arm as she hastened to introduce them.

'Ralph, this is Guy Maitland, the son of my late father's business partner. Mr Maitland, this is Ralph Brentwood, the brother of my dear school friend, who is now Lady Westlake.'

The two men bowed again, in acknowledgement of the introduction.

Emily knew it was not the time to explain what had happened. She laid her hand on Ralph's arm and smiled up at him. 'I was so entranced by all of this that I became separated from everyone and didn't know which way to go. Mr Maitland came to my rescue and was about to bring me to you.' She turned to Mr Maitland again, holding out her hand. 'Thank you kindly for your assistance, sir. I hope we may meet again sometime.'

'I hope so, too,' he replied, gallantly

bowing over her hand and raising it to his lips. He straightened, making a brief bow to Ralph. 'Brentwood.'

Ralph found himself glaring at the man and realised he was being churlish. There was no doubt that the sight of Emily's hand laid so trustingly on the man's arm had caused his stomach to knot, and his first instinct had been to rush down the stairs and knock him over! It was as well he had not. The man had simply come to Miss Harcourt's rescue and he supposed he must be grateful. He returned the bow and then patted Emily's hand that lay still on his arm — *just where it ought to be*, he inwardly growled.

He turned, drawing Emily around with him, disliking the way she glanced over her shoulder smiling her farewell to the bounder, and began to lead her up the stairs. 'The first act has started,' he warned her, 'but you will not have missed much. I will explain if you find you cannot follow the plot.'

The box into which he led her

seemed to be already full, but Ralph ushered her through to the front row of seats and gestured for her to sit in the only unoccupied seat on that row. It was next to the one occupied by Miss Tildsley, who openly scowled and snapped her fan shut in annoyance.

'Is that not your seat?' Emily hissed at him.

'It is all right. As it is your first visit to the theatre, you must have a good seat. I shall sit behind you.' Which he did, leaning forward between her and Miss Tildsley to make brief comments as the play progressed.

It took Emily a while to compose herself, and she tried to concentrate on what was happening on the stage, but it was not easy. The audience felt under no obligation to listen quietly to the words being declared with passion by the thespians. They continued to converse loudly among themselves, even calling out to others further away, commenting loudly on the level of acting skills and laughing uproariously at each other's wit.

As the curtain closed at the end of the first act, she glanced around the dimly lit auditorium. Many others were doing the same, delighting in the mass of colour of elaborate clothing and sparkling jewellery. Opposite them, she could see some gentlemen openly ogling the ladies through their pince-nez or eye-glass. One had the audacity to stand up and bow in her direction and she hastily looked away in order to discourage such blatant behaviour. She had had quite enough excitement for one night!

A hot wave of shame washed over her as she remembered the scene in the foyer, thankful that neither Ralph nor Camilla had witnessed it. Oh! Was that why the man opposite had made so blatant a bow to her? Her cheeks flushed with heat. When Ralph asked if she would like to promenade during the interval, she vehemently declined.

Miss Tildsley immediately rose from her seat, touching his arm in an intimate gesture. She smiled into his eyes. 'I would be delighted to promenade with you, Mr Brentwood. I am sure I saw someone I know waving to me across the auditorium — an old friend whom I was hoping to meet whilst in Town. I would so like to speak to her.'

Ralph bowed his assent and led Miss Tildsley from the box.

A couple of others in their party chose to remain seated and under cover of the light conversations, Emily cautiously glanced over the auditorium and the other boxes to see if she could ascertain where her aunt and cousin were seated. She saw no sign of them. Maybe they had gone straight home after the incident? She did not wish to come face-to-face with them at the end of the performance. She knew they would delight in repeating their malicious remarks, hoping to shame her in front of her new-found friends.

The incident had shaken her more than she had realised at the time and, by the end of the performance, she was in a state of nervous anxiety as the audience rose to their feet to stamp and cheer and shout out to the bowing company of actors and actresses. She would be glad to return home.

She knew that Mr Maitland's timely intervention had prevented a worse outcome and she wished she had had time to thank him more profusely. She hoped she might see him again to assure him that, whatever his circumstances, she bore him no ill will and, if he were hoping to make a prestigious marriage, she would do nothing to harm his prospects.

Everyone began to gather their belongings — muffs or reticules for the ladies; hats, gloves and canes for the gentlemen — and made for the exits, clustering in groups as they emerged onto the crowded street, exchanging the mixed scents of smoke, perfume and perspiration of the theatre for the swirl of cold air, laden with the scent of horses and their droppings.

Hooves rang on the cobbled road and harnesses jangled; gentlemen's voices called out, 'Over here, man!' to their coachmen and, 'This way, ladies!' to their parties. People stepped aside to accommodate those fortunate enough to have their carriages arrive among the first few and then jostled back to regain their groupings, endeavouring to stay together. Emily, especially, had no wish to become separated from her party again.

She was uncomfortably pressed between two or three of the young men who were striving to keep their party together and, at the same time, keep a look-out for their carriage. She wriggled from between them and found herself on the fringe of her group. She gulped in a breath of air. Someone was trying to get back onto the flagway, murmuring 'Excuse me! Excuse me!' Emily tried to step aside but found herself once wedged in the crush.

The coachman on the carriage in front of them flicked his whip over the heads of his team and the carriage jerked into motion. Another was ready to take its place.

Emily heard someone say, ‘Ah, ours at last!’ and she turned to glance at the carriage that was approaching. In the dark, she had no idea whether it were one of the Westlake carriages or not, but she couldn’t resist standing on tip-toe to see if she could identify it.

The next moment, she felt something thud into the middle of her back between her shoulders and she began to fall forward. Her hands flailed ineffectively against the air but there was nothing to clutch hold of. She was falling face down into the cobbled roadway, right in the path of the approaching carriage.

8

At the last moment before hitting the cobbled road, Emily felt herself somehow scooped against a firm body that twisted her around as they fell entwined together, so that when she landed with a thud that winded her, she was not on the hard road.

Time seemed to stand still. She was aware that the back of her head was resting on something firm covered in fabric. She forced her eyes open. Anxious faces loomed overhead, looking down at her.

'Emily! Thank goodness you're all right!'

It was Camilla. As her friend's face swam in and out of focus, Emily began to struggle to sit up. As she did so, she heard Camilla cry out, 'Ralph! Open your eyes!'

Camilla dropped to her knees at

Emily's side and was gently patting the cheeks of the man lying on the ground beside her. Emily looked at him in bewilderment. His eyes were closed but she could tell from the rise and fall of his chest that he was still breathing. She realised her head had been nestling against his chest.

'What happened? Did I fall?'

'You seemed to stumble into the roadway, right into the path of the next carriage,' Camilla told her, as she gently lifted her brother's head. 'Ralph leaped forward and managed to drag you back. Has anyone got something I can put under my brother's head?'

'Here, allow me to do that, Camilla.' It was her husband. He dropped to his knees and pushed something under Ralph's head. 'He's all right. He's coming round. Stand back, everyone, and let him get some air.'

Philip Wraxley helped Camilla to stand. He had been further along the line of carriages, trying to pick out the position of their carriages when he had realised something was amiss.

'Do you think you are able to stand, Miss Harcourt?' he then asked.

'I believe so.' Emily took hold of his extended hand, allowing him to draw her to her feet. She felt unsteady and was glad of his supporting arm.

A groan and incoherent mumble from Ralph drew everyone's gaze and relief was felt all round when Ralph struggled to sit up.

'Oh, you poor man!' Miss Tildsley emerged from the crowd of bystanders and flung herself down beside him, sobbing hysterically against his chest. 'Oh, I thought you were dead! Let me hold you!'

'The carriage is here, Miss Tildsley. Allow me to assist you to rise,' Lord Westlake intervened, taking hold of her shoulders. 'We need to get Mr Brentwood and Miss Harcourt somewhere more congenial.'

'Let me stay with him!' Miss Tildsley pleaded, gripping tightly to the lapels of his coat. 'He needs me! We are almost betrothed, you know!'

'I am sorry, Miss Tildsley. Mr Brentwood must be taken to a physician who will be able to assess his condition,' Lord Westlake said firmly.

Camilla firmly disentangled Miss Tildsley's hands from Ralph's coat and, with the help of Miss Appleton, drew her to her feet. 'Our carriage is the one behind. Come along, my dear. We will be home in no time at all.'

Jack helped Ralph to his feet. He looked dazed but was able to stagger towards the carriage with the help of his brother-in-law and Mr Wraxley. As soon as the three men were seated, the carriage drew smoothly away.

Emily saw there was blood staining the folded coat that had been placed under his head. She realised that his speedy action had shielded her head from striking the ground and had saved her from a similar fate. She felt humbly grateful.

'Come in the next carriage with us, Emily,' Camilla encouraged her. 'The others will sort themselves out. Would you prefer to lie down?'

Her eyes were anxious and Emily hastened to reassure her. 'I am unhurt. Ralph took the force of the fall.'

'Your carelessness caused a nasty accident!' Miss Tildsley said sharply, dabbing her lace handkerchief to her eyes.

'It was an accident,' Camilla asserted firmly. 'There is no one to blame.'

'Well, I think there is!' Miss Tildsley persisted, glaring at Emily.

Emily leaned her head against the backrest and closed her eyes. She did not want the indignity of a heated argument over what had happened. Her mind was clearing, and she was remembering the last few moments before she fell. She had not intended to step forward; something had propelled her into the road . . . and that 'something' had been the firm thrust of a hand!

But who would want to push her into the road under the hooves of the horses or the carriage wheels? The only people in the vicinity who wished her ill were her aunt and cousin — but did they now hate her so much that they would attempt to injure her, or even cause her death? With a sinking heart, she realised it must be so.

* * *

The house party was subdued for a couple of days. Camilla summoned their physician to examine Emily and he proclaimed nothing more amiss than would be expected from such a fall.

'Of course, her inner organs will be somewhat shaken and will need time to settle — but she will recover after a few days' rest,' he declared.

Emily was happy to comply. She felt unaccountably tearful. As well as being shaken by her fall, she had been shocked by Miss Tildsley's assertion that she and Ralph were almost betrothed — even though she had been preparing herself for such an eventuality. She did not feel able to ask Camilla for confirmation, and Camilla made no mention of it herself.

That, and Ralph's own time of recuperation, meant that Emily felt she could share neither her conviction that she had been pushed into the road, nor her desire to meet with Mr Maitland in the near future in order to assure him of her understanding of his precarious position in Society.

On the third day after the unfortunate incident outside the Theatre Royal, Emily declared herself well-rested and allowed Jenny to help her to dress in a pretty day gown and arrange her hair in soft ringlets. Camilla came to escort her down the stairs.

'And we have had word from Ralph, this morning, Emily,' Camilla was pleased to impart. 'He sent a messenger round with a short note, assuring us that he is much recovered and will rejoin us in a few days. That is good news, is it not? Jack tells me he had a lump the size of a goose egg on the back of his head and it is still very tender. I think he is waiting until the bandages have been removed before he shows himself in public again!'

The other young people welcomed Emily back amongst them. Her pleasant, unassuming manner had made her popular and only Miss Tildsley tried to make her feel inferior in their company.

'Take no notice of Miss Tildsley!' whispered a quiet girl called Lucinda Gresham. 'She would have us believe that she has an understanding with Mr Brentwood but no one else has mentioned an imminent betrothal. I think we may take it to be a bag of moonshine, don't you?'

Emily did not dare let herself be too comforted by Lucinda's opinion, even though she had no real hopes of reclaiming Ralph's affections for herself. If she could choose the one to win Ralph's affections, she favoured Lucinda above the others, but felt it wise not to say so, since she had no desire to make the girl feel self-conscious about it.

It was a fine day and after luncheon

was over, everyone agreed that a drive in Hyde Park would be the very thing. The ladies presented a pretty picture in their carriage dresses and matching parasols. Their carriages made slow progress as most of the haut ton were driving, riding or promenading in the Park and many stops were made in order to exchange greetings and bestow compliments.

Emily was glad that Camilla had invited her into her carriage. Lord Westlake was driving. She delighted in gazing around and watched in amazement at the way some dandies were openly ogling the ladies and eyeing other bucks. 'They are making sure no one else's clothes outclass their own!' she laughed to Camilla. 'They certainly think a lot of themselves!'

As they drove on, Emily recognised a tall, slender figure riding towards them on a magnificent chestnut. He had a good seat and was attracting admiring glances.

'There is Mr Maitland!' she exclaimed.

She turned tell Camilla who he was and to ask if it would be proper for her to speak with him — but, when she turned back to gesture to him to approach the carriage, she realised that he had changed direction and was riding away.

'He cannot have seen us,' she said, disappointed. 'I was sure he had.'

Camilla frowned, perfectly sure that the young man Emily had indicated had indeed noticed them. 'How well do you know him?' she asked.

'Not at all, really,' Emily confessed, 'though I had hoped to speak with him, to thank him for his assistance at the theatre the other night.'

'Was he there when you fell? I do not remember seeing him.'

'No, it was earlier. I did not tell you as it seemed so unimportant after Ralph had been so badly injured.' She grimaced, as she went on to describe the embarrassing scene her aunt and Juliana had caused. 'Mr Maitland overheard and rescued me. He was going to take me to your box but then

Ralph came. I did not really thank him properly. I fear he may be in similar straits as I am. After all, his father was ruined financially when my papa was.'

'He does not look like someone at low ebb,' Camilla commented. 'That chestnut seems a fine bit of blood.'

'He may be putting on a brave face,' Emily pointed out. 'Look at me. Everyone must think I am quite an heiress.'

'No, they do not. Anyone who matters knows you are my friend and accepts you as such. You are making no claim to be anything you are not.' She studied her friend's face. 'Are you concerned about him, dear?'

'A little,' Emily confessed. 'It must be even harder for a man to have to make his way with no fortune.'

'I shall ask Jack to make some discreet enquiries about him,' Camilla promised. 'Then we shall know if your concern about him is necessary. Now, since he has gone the other way, let us enjoy the rest of our drive. Would you like to alight and walk for a while? We can wander to the bank of the Serpentine and see if there are any ducks there. They are so sweet when they have their families of babies with them!'

Emily felt relieved to have shared her concern over Mr Maitland with Camilla, for she had been unable to think of a way to contact him without overstepping the bounds of propriety — and she knew of no way to make discreet enquiries about anyone, whereas Lord Westlake would know just the way to go about it without upsetting Mr Maitland's precarious position.

* * *

Nothing more was said of the matter over the next few days and Emily threw herself into enjoying the activities Camilla had planned for the entertainment of her guests. During the daytime, they had drives into the country; shopping expeditions along Oxford

Street that usually ended with delicious ices at Gunter's confectioner's shop in Berkley Square; and visits to the historical sights of London. And in the evenings, there were more visits to the theatre and private balls and routs.

Everyone cheered when Ralph made his reappearance amongst them. He seemed none the worse and declared his wound completely healed.

'I do thank you for saving me as you did,' Emily told him at the earliest opportunity, 'though I am sorry it led to you being injured in my stead.'

'I was happy to do it,' Ralph assured her. 'My heart nearly stopped when I realised you were falling into the road.'

His eyes displayed such caring that Emily's breath caught in her throat. 'I am glad you were there,' she breathed. She had already decided not to mention the possibility that she might have been pushed. A week had gone by and no one had come forward to say that they had noticed any such action — and she felt the matter was best left alone.

The corners of his eyes crinkled as he smiled. 'So am I!'

No more was said, but Emily felt a happy glow spread through her body. Her acceptance among Camilla's house guests bolstered her confidence and she felt more relaxed in Ralph's company. At times, she even felt that their former friendship was being restored, though Ralph still shared his time and attention amongst all the young ladies — as did the other young men of the party. But Emily was happy to note that she received her fair share.

Her favourite moments were when they danced together. She had quickly learned how to waltz, and loved the swift turns and the sensation of floating on air whenever she participated in that particular dance. Especially when partnered by Ralph.

One afternoon, Camilla drew Emily into her private sitting room and sat next to her on the sofa. She did not prevaricate, but took hold of Emily's hands and said gently, 'Jack has made some enquiries about Guy Maitland. It appears that his father, Mr Walter Maitland, is reasonably wealthy and still runs his shipping business in Bristol. It apparently had some sort of crisis a few years ago but he swiftly recovered.'

Emily gasped in surprise. 'But he told my father he was completely ruined! He refused to give him any help whatsoever to tide him over until he could find a new backer.'

'Then he either lied, or found a new backer himself and was fortunate in subsequent ventures,' Camilla asserted. 'What exactly went wrong? Did your father take you into his confidence?'

Emily shook her head. 'I do not know the details. Mama was under the impression that a ship carrying a valuable cargo, into which Papa had invested all his capital, was lost in high seas, and it was uninsured. Papa said Mr Maitland was supposed to have arranged that, but Mr Maitland said it was Papa's responsibility. I think that is why he took his own life, because people were saying it was his fault. But it was not. Papa would never have lied about it.'

'Hmm! Well, it seems Mr Guy Maitland is a big spender — but tales are being whispered that he is sailing very close to the wind and is, in fact, borrowing money in order to maintain his lavish lifestyle. Until this Season, it seems he has been content to dazzle the provinces, but he is already at a standstill in London — and is getting a name for not honouring his vowels.' She paused, than added thoughtfully, 'Tell me, was the partnership between your father and Mr Maitland senior ever legally ended?'

Emily shook her head. 'I do not know. Mama couldn't face the shame of it all and we simply got what we could for our home and went to live in seclusion in Cheshire. We managed to buy a small cottage, and lived there until Mama died. There was nothing left by that time and I threw myself on Aunt Augusta's mercy. I imagine the partnership would have ended with Papa's death, would it not?'

'Maybe. It might be worth Jack making more enquiries, though. I shall get him to look into it. Whatever the outcome of that, I think you should be very wary of associating yourself with him. All in all, he did you a big favour by not approaching you in the park the other day.'

Emily nodded soberly. At least it showed Mr Maitland had some fine feelings left to him!

* * *

Emily would have probably left it at that. Apart from Mr Maitland's gallantry in rescuing her from Aunt Augusta's verbal onslaught at the theatre, he had not impressed her a great deal. He had been offhand with her at Lady Blanford's ball once he had learned her identity, and had cut her in the park. Now that she knew he was not living an impoverished life, she felt no need to assure him of her decision not to spread whispers about him. It seemed he was managing very well on his own.

The following day, however, when visiting an art gallery with most of the younger members of the house party, Emily felt a light touch on her arm.

She was startled to see that it was Juliana. It was not a meeting that Emily desired and she immediately took a step away, hastily looking about her for someone she recognised — but none was there. Belatedly she realised that she had lingered behind the others to fully appreciate the oil painting on the wall in front of her, allowing the others to move on without her. She immediately turned away, intending to hurry after her party. They were in the next room. She would soon be with them.

'Emily! Wait!' Juliana hissed, reaching out to her again. The girl was clearly agitated and, though she feared a repetition of insults, Emily felt compelled to halt.

'What is it, Juliana? Are you here on your own? Or is Aunt Augusta with you? I have no wish to meet her after her performance the other night!'

'That's what it is about,' Juliana pleaded. 'Mama wants to apologise to you.' She glanced around, as if anxious not to be overheard. 'She did not mean what she said. She was upset. Things have not been going well and she . . . well, when she saw you in such fine company it turned her a little mad. But she's sorry now. She wishes to apologise. You will come, won't you? She'll be cross with me if you don't! I did not agree with what she said the other night. We had an awful row later. It will take but a moment.'

Emily hesitated. She did not wish to see her aunt, but supposed she ought to allow her to clear her conscience by apologising. 'Very well; I'll just let my friends know where I'm going.'

She took a step towards the next room, but Juliana grasped her arm. 'There's no need. It will not take a minute. She is in a carriage just outside. We saw you come in with your friends, and she sent me to speak to you. Only the horses are getting restless. It is a hired cab and the driver is not very pleased about stopping there.'

Emily was reluctant to go with Juliana but it seemed churlish to refuse. With a last glance over her shoulder towards the doorway to the next room, she turned and hurried back towards the front entrance at Juliana's side.

'I'll be re-entering in a few moments,' she said to the commissionaire who stood on duty at the entrance.

'Very well, miss.'

Emily paused on the top step. Sure enough, a hired cab waited at the kerbside. The side curtains were drawn and Emily presumed her aunt did not wish to be seen. Drawing a deep breath, she followed Juliana.

There was no groom to hold open the door but Juliana performed that duty, unhooking the step so that it fell forward, then stepped back, holding the door. She nodded towards the interior. 'She's in there!'

Emily felt a vague unease as she picked up her skirt and stepped up into the carriage. In the dim interior, she discerned a figure seated in the corner.

'Aunt Augusta?' she queried hesitantly.

The figure moved swiftly, grasping hold of her arm and pulling her forward. At the same time, she heard the clang of the step being dropped back into its position for travelling and the door was slammed shut. Immediately, the carriage jerked forward, throwing Emily against the rear-facing seat. Whoever the other person in the carriage was, it certainly was not her aunt!

9

Trying to stand up in the swaying carriage, Emily shouted, 'Hey! Who are you? What do you think you are doing? Stop the carriage and let me out at once!'

'I advise you to sit down before you suffer another nasty fall,' a male voice said calmly. 'And before you think of trying to leap from the carriage, let me warn you that if the fall does not kill you, a bullet from my pistol will!'

Emily was stunned into silence. She could see the glint of the dark metal shape in her abductor's hand. She sank onto the seat and stared intently at the figure in the corner. Suddenly she knew who he was. 'You are Mr Maitland, are you not? I know not why you are doing this, but I warn you to stop at once and let me out! My friends will already be alerting the authorities to my absence.

If you return me now, we will think of some way to resolve the matter.'

Mr Maitland laughed. 'No one will have missed you yet. By the time they do, we will be far away — and no one knows where we are going, not even your foolish cousin who so obligingly brought you to me. I advise you to do exactly as I tell you. This pistol is loaded, and I will use it if necessary.'

'But *why?*' Emily demanded. She was afraid, but not yet desperately so. She could not believe that the man intended to do any harm to her. What reason had he to do so? It had to be some sort of wager — he had bet someone he could abduct her and hoped to gain some financial benefit.

'You were getting too nosy,' Mr Maitland coolly informed her. 'And after your veiled threats at the theatre, I decided that I needed to be rid of you.'

'Veiled threats?' Emily echoed, not yet taking in the remainer of his words. 'I made no veiled threats. What are you talking about?'

'You said you had things to discuss with me; things to sort out, regarding our fathers' business affairs. You have obviously discovered that half my father's fortune belongs to you. I knew, then, that I had to get rid of you, though I acted hastily that evening. I had not worked out that I could benefit even more financially from a different method of getting rid of you!'

Emily's eyes widened. 'It was you who pushed me? You could have killed me!'

'That was the idea, my dear — but, on reflection, I am glad I failed. There is a more profitable way.'

Emily was shocked. 'But why? I am no threat to you.'

'Oh, but you are, my dear — and someone has been poking about in my affairs! That was you, was it not? You or your wealthy titled friends! 'I'm with Lord and Lady Westlake's party!' ' he mimicked. 'Letting me know you have friends with influence. Well, they'll do you no good where I'm taking you!'

'But you were mistaken!' Emily

whispered. 'I felt concerned about you. I believed you to be impoverished by our fathers' failure in business, as I was, and that you hoped to marry someone with money in order to better yourself. I wished merely to tell you I would not spread tales about you.'

'Ha! Is that your aim? To marry someone with money? Is that why you are hanging on to Brentwood's sleeve? He's flush in the pocket all right. You should have been content with that, instead of trying to bleed money out of me. Or, more likely, out of my father, since I expect your friends have discovered that I'm on the rocks.

'Well, you need not think I'm willing to share half my inheritance with you.' His voice became harder, with a vindictive edge to it. 'I've waited long enough, having it doled out in miserly handfuls, to give it up now. As soon as the old man snuffs it, I'll be out of dun territory and able to live it up, at last.' He laughed harshly. 'So you do see why I have to get rid of you? Nothing personal, of course. Let us just say you made your move at the wrong time.'

Emily sank back against the seat rest. Half of his father's money was rightfully hers? Mr Maitland had let her papa believe he had been the means of ruining their business, when he had not — and then let her mama and her live in poverty. But what good was all that to her now?

'I did not even know you had money,' she said reasonably. 'Nor that your father had made a recovery from the loss of *The Pelican*. Just tell the coachman to turn around, and we'll forget this has ever happened.'

'You must take me for a fool, Miss Harcourt. Besides, all is arranged. A certain sea captain I know is sailing for the Caribbean in twenty-four hours' time — and you, my pretty maid, will be sailing with him. It's quite a lucrative trade. I'll get a few hundred guineas for an untouched maid like you.'

Emily stared at him, utterly appalled. 'You must be insane!' She summoned some reserve of strength. 'I won't go!'

'You will have no choice. The trade route is already established — tavern-keepers' palms already greased. You are not the first to come this way, my dear, and neither will you be the last. We cross the river at Dartford, then on to Rochester where we will stop for the night; and then to Rushenden quay for the morning tide, and a sea trip that will change your life for ever. A fate worse than death, I believe you ladies think of it — but I am sure you will grow accustomed to it. You may even enjoy it. Some ladies do, you know.'

The calm revelation of his plan froze Emily's senses more than if he had dramatised it in a more lurid fashion. She knew she must stay calm, too. It would be her only chance of seizing an opportunity to escape.

* * *

In the art gallery, Ralph was searching for Emily. He had lingered with her through the first few rooms, before being drawn ahead by Miss Tildsley's insistence on his continued comparison of the styles of the eighteenth-century works of William Hogarth and Francis Hayman, whose works graced the supper boxes at Vauxhall and were hanging here in a special exhibition.

'Where is Miss Harcourt?' he wondered aloud.

'Oh, she was probably bored by these superior works of art and has summoned a cab to take her home,' Miss Tildsley suggested sweetly, running her fingers along his arm. 'After all, she has not the right sort of upbringing to appreciate the finer points of artistic works, has she?'

'Rubbish!' Ralph snapped, feeling a degree of alarm. 'She has a fine eye and was engrossed in the earlier paintings. Nor would she act so inconsiderately as to leave without informing us. I shall ask the doorman!'

Leaving Miss Tildsley speechless for once, he hurried to the entrance.

'Yes, sir! I do remember a young lady leaving, though she was not alone. She said she would return, but she got into a cab and was driven away. The other young lady did not accompany her, though. She walked away in that direction.' He pointed along the road.

'And the first young lady went in which direction?'

'The other way, sir. The carriage set off at a cracking pace, too! I remember thinking, 'Hey up, cabbie! Let the young lady take her seat!''

'What did the second young lady look like? How was she dressed?'

The commissionaire searched his memory. 'Not as stylish as your party, sir. Her gown was a sort of purple colour — not what you normally see on a young lady, if you know what I mean.'

Ralph nodded. None of their party was dressed in such a colour. But who else did Emily know well enough to feel at ease in leaving with them? Only that aunt and cousin of hers. Had there been a family crisis to which she had been summoned? Even so, he was sure Emily would not have left without giving word.

'Which of the young ladies said she was coming back? The one who was driven away?'

'That's right, sir. 'I'll be re-entering in a few moments,' is what she said. That's why I was surprised when the carriage shot away as it did. It was a hackney carriage, sir,' he added significantly.

'Yes, I see,' Ralph responded. As the commissionaire was aware, it was the sort of carriage someone of the upper classes would not choose unless forced to. It reinforced his thought that Emily might have been persuaded to visit her aunt — though whether willingly or unwillingly, he didn't know.

He returned inside and swiftly organised the remaining members of the party to return to the Westlakes' residence, drawing Philip Wraxley aside.

'Get hold of Jack. Tell him what has happened, and that I am visiting Miss Harcourt's aunt to discover what she might know of the situation. Tell him that I fear it may concern a certain person we have been investigating — though I am hoping not! Jack will know what I mean. If I am right, we will have to inform the Runners of this latest development. Tell Jack to prepare a couple of carriages to journey to the coast, and to send a messenger to my groom to have Jupiter saddled and ready for me. Meet at my place as soon as everything is ready — oh, and warn him we may need firearms!'

He then walked swiftly to the side road where he knew the coachmen were walking the horses. His coachman spotted him immediately and swung up onto the driving seat. Ralph would have preferred to busy himself with the task of driving but knew he was too agitated to negotiate the London traffic with consideration for other vehicles. His mind whirled over the information Jack's investigators had imparted, thumping a fist into the other palm. They should have moved sooner! He still hoped he was mistaken; hoped that there was a more straightforward explanation, but he doubted it.

He rapped the door knocker of the Simmons' residence with a ferocity that should have caused the lace curtains of neighbouring houses to twitch.

When the door opened, he thrust his way past the startled footman without ceremony.

'I — I'll announce you, Mr Brentwood,' the footman stammered, following him along the hall to the drawing room, 'though Mrs Simmons has guests.'

'I'll announce myself!' Ralph said tersely. 'Wait out here!'

He thrust the door open without knocking and strode inside, disregarding the startled faces that swung his way. He bowed curtly. 'Ladies!'

His eyes were searching for Mrs Simmons, but it was the reaction of her daughter that took his attention. After a moment of frozen shock, the girl's face blanched of all colour and she leaped to her feet, spilling the plate of tiny pastries onto the carpet as she backed away. She was still attired in the unbecoming purple gown.

Mrs Simmons also rose, her face livid and her voice trembling with indignation. 'Mr Brentwood! I do not believe you were invited to my salon!'

'No, ma'am,' Ralph agreed calmly, his eyes still upon Juliana. 'I beg you will accept my apology for intruding. I have urgent need to speak with Miss Simmons. Is there a private room we may use?'

'No, Mama! I won't speak with him!' Juliana cried, her hands twisting the napkin she held. 'I know not what he wants!'

'I think you do, Miss Simmons. You were seen — and recognised!'

'I wasn't! No-one saw me! He's lying! I feel faint! Tell him to go, Mama!'

'I have no time to pander to your sensibilities, Miss Simmons. This is a matter of life and death. Tell me, who was in the carriage into which you lured Miss Harcourt?'

He disregarded the gasps and shocked

faces around him. 'I demand an answer, Miss Simmons. Your cousin's life may depend upon it!'

Juliana glanced frantically from side to side but saw only hostile, expectant faces.

'Don't resort to hysterics, miss!' Ralph said sharply, correctly interpreting the calculating glimmer in her eyes. 'A name. Then I will go.'

'Juliana?' Mrs Simmons said faintly, her hands fluttering nervously at the base of her neck. 'Do you know what he wants?'

'No, Mama! Really, I — '

'Life or death, Miss Simmons!' Ralph reminded her. 'You will be held accountable if you persist in this charade.'

Juliana gulped, her face now flushing with colour. 'It was Mr Maitland,' she muttered. 'He said it was a game. He said I wouldn't be implicated.'

'Thank you, Miss Simmons. Do not leave town in the next few days. Ladies!' He bowed curtly and left.

His worst fear had been confirmed.

10

Leaving the Simmons' residence, Ralph hurried to his own home and bellowed for his valet as he leaped up the staircase two steps at a time. Westlake arrived before he had completely changed into his riding clothes.

'Maitland's got her!' Ralph said tersely.

Jack nodded. 'I suspected as much from the message you sent.'

'Did you send word to Colonel Grantham to gather a group of militia?'

'Yes. Thank goodness we liased with him the other day when we uncovered the details of his vile trade. I did not expect this, though! I just hope Grantham's men have managed to identify his likely handover point. We've no time for mistakes. He will want to pass her on before anyone can link her abduction to him.'

'Let us hope he expects her to fetch a price too high to trust her to anyone but himself. We need to nail him — not just his underlings!'

'I have people looking for him. If he returns to town, he'll be spotted.'

'Good . . . but I hope it is an unnecessary precaution. I want to be the one who gets him.' Ralph took his hat from his valet. 'Let's be going!'

'Are you armed?'

'Yes.'

* * *

Colonel Grantham had been busy since the valuable information had landed in his hands so opportunely. In spite of mounting evidence indicating that a number of abducted vulnerable young women, mostly from the backstreet slums of the city, were being sold to foreign clients who then smuggled them out of the country, never to be seen again, no one had been able, or willing, to divulge a name. Not until the other day.

Since then, a careful watch had been kept on a certain young man-about-town. His movements had been noted and the net had begun to tighten around him — but not soon enough, it seemed.

Maitland's departure from town with a lady of quality did not exactly fit the pattern of previous abductions. She had been seen to step into Maitland's hired carriage with only a slight hesitation, and the man on surveillance duty might have assumed it to be no more than a social engagement, had not the carriage then set off at a reckless pace. The undercover militiaman lost no time in passing on the information, and the carriage was later seen to be heading eastward towards the coast.

When Lord Westlake's urgent message reached him, Colonel Grantham knew his men's vigilance had paid off. By the time Westlake and his friend met up with his hastily rounded-up contingent of armed officers, more confirmation had been passed on to him.

'They are heading in the direction of Gravesend and the Medway, your lordship,' he was happy to announce. 'But we do not yet know if he'll head along the northern bank or the southern one. I am alerting the coastguards to let any likely vessel slip inshore without challenge — but it will not slip out quite so easily. We will catch him in the act, have no fear!'

'How far ahead are they?' Ralph asked.

'Two to three hours,' Grantham replied. 'My men have orders to keep watch only until we see how the land lies. They will move in only if there is any indication of an earlier embarkation, though I doubt that as the next high tide is in the early hours of tomorrow. I wish to catch Maitland in the act of handing the lady over; then there will be no let-out for him — and less chance of others getting hurt. We will make no move until we have all escape routes covered. This is one blackguard who won't get away!'

It was dusk by the time the mounted party reached the coast. They then swung northeast, along a sparsely inhabited route, past Hoo and a series of hamlets until the road beneath the pounding hooves deteriorated into a surface that could only be described as a track. Colonel Grantham checked the positions of his men at each crossroads and ascertained the time the carriage had reached that point.

'We are no more than half an hour behind them,' was the final estimation, 'but they will have gone to ground for the night by the time we arrive.'

He was right. They skirted round the edge of a small village set back from the shore and left their horses in a derelict barn in the care of a couple of militia men. From a vantage point, it was plain to see that the track now led only to the shore. Under the cover of the deepening shadows of dusk, they moved silently forward until they were in sight of an old tavern on the stone jetty. No lights were showing but, at their approach, a man rose from the side of a hillock to reassure them that the hired carriage had deposited its passengers and was now secreted in one of the smaller buildings along the jetty. None seemed to be occupied.

'The tale goes that the part of the village by the jetty was wiped out in a storm nearly a century ago,' the colonel said quietly, as he rejoined Ralph and Jack, lying on their stomachs overlooking the inlet. 'According to a local informant, stories of ghosts circulated years ago and have resurfaced recently, presumably to keep intruders away — and explain any sightings that may have occurred. Also, recently, sea-going vessels have been seen near shore; some are known to have tied up at the jetty for short periods at high tide. I think we can assume a ship is due in the next few hours.'

Ralph's mind slipped back into his military role in the Peninsular War. If there were only enemy personnel in the tavern, the plan would be simple. Surround and attack. But with at least one innocent civilian in there, it would be a risky tactic. Even so, he could not stop himself asking, 'Have we enough men to surround the place? Are we moving in?'

He could not bear to think of Emily being in captivity for a moment longer than necessary. Why had he delayed so long in letting her know that he still loved her? Was it because he was unsure if she loved him? He had begun to hope she did. What if he now never got the chance to tell her?

He was unsurprised by Colonel Grantham's reply. 'I do not wish to attack in the dark. There would be too much risk of stray bullets hitting the wrong targets. We'll wait until daybreak. My captain will set a watch and the rest of us will bed down for the night in the old barn.'

It was not easy to turn away from their target, but he knew the colonel's decision was the best one available to them. Consequently, he wrapped himself up in his saddle-blanket and, for a few cold, uncomfortable hours, tossed in restless slumber.

⋆ ⋆ ⋆

Emily awoke the following morning aching throughout her body.

Last evening, under the threat of Maitland's pistol, she had been hustled from the carriage into a dark tavern. They appeared to have arrived at a small seashore hamlet and her frantic glances around had shown her that a stone jetty lay across from the tavern, though no vessel was tied up there at present. The noise of raucous laughter and drunken voices gave her no hope of gaining assistance from any of the tavern's clientele.

'Remember, I will shoot you if you try to escape!' Maitland reminded her. 'I gain by your death anyway and will only lose the price of your sale.'

He nodded to a man who was leaning against the door jamb of the open door. The man levered himself upright and sauntered over, leering at Emily.

'Got a good looker, 'ere, mister! Wouldn't mind a shilling's worth myself!'

'Keep your filthy hands off this one. Just hand me that length of rope so that I can secure her!'

He tucked the pistol into his waistband, grabbed her arms, twisted her round and fastened her wrists together behind her back. He then hustled her into the tavern and handed her over to a slatternly dressed woman, who dragged her up a flight of stairs and thrust her into a sparsely furnished room. There was a wooden chair and an iron-framed bed with some grey-looking covers on it and a chamber pot on the floor.

'Not quite what you're used to,' the woman sneered, 'but you'll be thankful for what you get from now on.'

'How can you do this?' Emily pleaded. 'Have you no compassion?'

'No one never 'ad any fer me,' the woman responded flatly. 'Yer teks what yer can if yer want to survive.' She pushed Emily towards the bed. 'I'll untie yer 'ands later when I've someone to watch over yer. Yer'd best lie down until then. And it's no use wasting yer strength shouting fer help. There's no one to 'ear yer.'

Emily felt she were in the midst of a living nightmare. She tried hard not to despair. She could not quite believe that Guy Maitland meant what he threatened. Were men so depraved that someone would buy an unwilling woman of gentle birth?

She squeezed her eyes closed and shook the thought from her mind: she must remain positive.

Instead, she thought of Ralph. He had seemed so much more tender towards her of late and she had begun to feel that, given time, there was hope of renewing their former closeness. He would miss her. He would search for her . . . . but how would he find her? No one would think to search this far from London.

An image of his face imprinted itself on her inner mind — and some words he had spoken seemed to echo back to her. 'Hold on to your dreams!' he had said. That's what she must do. She could not lose hope. She could not!

But, in the cold grey light of morning, it was hard to hold on to that thought. She had suffered the indignity of having to use the chamber pot under the sneering gaze of her jailer and, although she had attempted to eat the food that had been brought to her before her hands were once more tied behind her, her throat had refused to swallow it.

A seagoing vessel was now tied up to the jetty. She heard a shout from outside and the woman who stood guard over her remarked, 'It's here! Say goodbye to England, missie! You'll never see its shore again!'

Maitland swaggered into the room.

'Time to be off and away, my sweetie!' he announced with false gaiety. 'I hope you are not going to make a fuss, though I have had a number of offers to carry you on board if necessary! It's your choice, of course. Shall we go?'

He made a courtly bow before grasping hold of her right arm just above her elbow and hustling her out of the room in front of him. She almost stumbled going down the dark stairway. Her heart was thudding and she was afraid her legs would give way beneath her. She was very afraid. She knew her only hope of escaping would be to make the attempt once she was out of the tavern but before she was on board the ship.

'Help me, please!' she urged the slatternly woman who had kept guard over her. But her appeal fell on unresponsive ears. The woman was hardened by poverty and her own harsh existence. What did one more or one less genteelly-reared young woman matter to her?

Emily stumbled over the threshold into the chilly morning air. Her heart quailed. The sailing ship was no more than twenty feet away across the quayside. A swarthy sailor stood on deck, his legs wide and his hands on his hips. He shouted a comment in a foreign tongue followed by a coarse bellow of a laugh.

Emily did not need to understand the words to feel a deep humiliation. A wave of heat flooded over her face. This was unbearable! However, she straightened her shoulders and looked Maitland in the eyes.

'I implore you, as an Englishman and a gentleman, not to do this. There must be another way!'

'None that pays so well, m'dear! Besides, I need to be rid of you — and, this way, at least you get to live!' He pushed her forward onto the cobbled quayside, still tightly grasping hold of her arm.

She was at the edge of the quay, at the foot of a wooden gangway, with Maitland still hustling her from behind, when a strong voice cut through the cold air.

'Stop right there, in the name of the King!'

Maitland reacted immediately. He took a step back, pulling Emily to stand in front of him, facing the direction from where the authoritative voice had come.

'Let her go, Maitland! We have the place surrounded!'

Emily could see a number of figures, some in military uniform and some in dark coats. They were clearly armed and a few riflemen began to advance, rifles at their shoulders, moving with a measured tread. She tried to pull away from Maitland but he was holding her too tightly. She felt the muzzle of a pistol press against her temple.

'I'll shoot her!' he called out. He began to drag her backwards towards the ship, intending to drag her up the gangway. From the shouts on board behind them, Emily sensed the sailors were cutting the ropes that bound them to the capstans.

Maitland must have realised it too and increased his pace. Emily resisted, straining away from him. Maitland stumbled. He sank backwards onto the wooden gangplank, still holding on to her. As he fell, his pistol fired. The noise seemed deafening in Emily's ear but she had no time to wonder if she had been hit.

Another shot rang out. Maitland scrabbled backwards, trying to get back on his feet whilst still holding on to Emily. She made herself fall against him in order to unbalance him again. He let out a shout and, in slow motion, it seemed, the two of them toppled off the gangplank. After a moment's sense of falling, they hit the surface of the water and sank down into the sea.

Ralph was already running across the quay. He cast his pistol to the ground and dragged his coat off as he ran. The gap between the boat and the quayside was widening. Ralph could see nothing in the water. He did not know how deep it was, save that it was deep enough for the keel of the ship. He dived in, forcing himself down, feeling with his hands, straining to see in the churning water.

He felt some fabric. He hoped it was Emily's gown. It had to be. It was too soft and flimsy to be male attire. He pulled it to him and grabbed hold of the firmer substance of a human body, and forced himself up to the surface, gasping for a breath of air.

'Over here, Ralph!' he heard Jack shout.

Jack was half way down some stone steps that led down from the quayside. Ralph kicked towards him, holding Emily's head against his chest, keeping her face above the water. Jack reached down and grabbed hold of her, hauling her out of the water as Ralph hauled himself out.

'Get back!' Jack shouted to the men

at the top of the steps. 'Make way!'

Willing hands helped to place Emily face down on the quayside. As they did so, her chest heaved, her stomach wretched and sea-water gushed from her mouth. Ralph sank down beside her.

'My love! Thank God! You're alive!'

* * *

Whilst Ralph and Jack were rescuing Emily, the captain of the ship had managed to cast off from the quayside and begin to make headway towards the open sea. Colonel Grantham contented himself with ordering a few volleys to be fired in its wake, knowing the excise men were waiting beyond the headland. He then directed his men to storm the tavern and detain anyone still inside.

They found four bedraggled young women locked in a room to the rear of the tavern, all much abused and fearful of their future existence in foreign brothels. Ralph ordered Emily's former jailer to clear the best room so that Emily could have somewhere to recover from her ordeal in privacy.

He carried her inside and bade the woman find some towelling and some dry clothing.

Emily clung to him. 'Don't leave me with her!' she begged.

'She will harm you at her peril,' Ralph assured her, glowering at the woman.

The woman hastily sketched a brief curtsey, fear for her own future taking over from her former callous attitude to Emily's plight. 'I meant no 'arm, miss,' she whined. 'I 'as to do as I'm told!'

'See to it, then!' Ralph curtly ordered. 'And then light a fire in the grate. Miss Harcourt needs warmth.'

The woman backed hastily from the room, murmuring, 'Yes, milord. Right away, milord.'

By the time she returned, Ralph had begun to massage some warmth into Emily's hands and arms and he relinquished his place with some reluctance, warning the woman, 'I shall be immediately outside the room.'

Later, garbed in an assortment of rough clothing, Emily self-consciously welcomed him back into the room. She felt frail and wretched but thankful to be safe. 'Was Maitland caught?' she asked anxiously, as Ralph seated himself on the edge of the pallet that served as a sofa, fearing even yet that Maitland might somehow return to attempt to abduct her.

Ralph took hold of her hands, now warm but still trembling. 'Maitland is dead,' he told her calmly. 'He must have banged his head as he fell. At least he was unconscious when he drowned — though the blackguard deserved all he got! If he had harmed you, I would have throttled him with my own hands!'

'He was so cold-hearted.' Emily shuddered. 'And he had no pity whatsoever. He intended to sell me,' she added with incredulity. 'I assured him I meant him no harm, but he seemed to think I was after half of his fortune. I did not know he had any. Why would I? I thought his father to be as impoverished as mine!'

'It seems Maitland senior defrauded your father of his share of their joint business enterprise,' Ralph told her. 'Jack instigated an investigation. The cargo that was supposedly lost at sea had, in fact, never been loaded before the doomed vessel set sail. It was a deliberate insurance fraud.'

'But the premium hadn't been paid,' Emily corrected him. 'Mr Maitland accused my father of negligence. It was that accusation that destroyed him, and shamed him into taking his own life.'

Ralph circled the pads of his thumbs over the backs of Emily's hands. 'It seems that the premium had indeed been paid, but under a different policy from that which your father knew about. Maitland received both the insurance money and the eventual sale price of the cargo.'

Emily felt distraught. 'The shame

killed both my parents,' she said bleakly. 'We were left with nothing.'

'Except your honour,' Ralph said quietly. 'And your father's honour will be restored. I have already set my lawyers to investigate the business and to determine whether or not you do indeed have claim to half of Maitland's present assets.'

Emily shook her head wonderingly. 'So, I may not be penniless after all. I may have enough money to live comfortably?'

'Indeed you might,' Ralph agreed, 'though I am hoping that that may be immaterial. My dearest Emily, this may not be the best of moments to declare my love for you — but when I realised what danger you were in, I wished with all of my heart that I had spoken more forcibly about my renewed feelings for you!'

Emily swallowed, hardly daring to grasp what he was saying. Ralph's eyes were earnestly scanning her face. Did he not realise that her feelings for him had never changed?

'Yes?' she encouraged him, smiling shyly, squeezing his fingers slightly.

'I love you, Emily. I always have — though I thought I had learned to let you go. I was mistaken, however. My love for you is as strong as ever it was! Can I hope that you still have feelings for me?'

Emily beamed at him. She let her breath sigh deeply out of her body. Ralph still loved her. Still wanted her.

There was one problem, however — a problem she feared he might have overlooked. 'But what about Miss Tildsley?' she asked anxiously, not wanting him to make a declaration only to have to retract it later. 'Will she not be very disappointed?'

'I doubt it. Not for long, anyway. I was careful to pay her no more attention than a few other young ladies. Besides, her mama will soon have another eligible party lined up for her to impress with her good breeding and sense of obligation.' He gave a self-deprecating laugh. 'Until I saw you again, I had the foolish notion that breeding and duty were the better qualities to seek in a prospective wife — safer than allowing my heart to love again. But, now I know differently. I love you, Emily, whether you will have me or not!'

This was no time for maidenly shilly-shallying. Their nerves were far too frayed by the traumatic events of the past 24 hours for that.

'I love you, too, Ralph,' she declared without further dissembling. 'My love for you never wavered. I just . . . well . . . pretended it had. My name was dishonoured. I felt I could not hold you to honour your pledge to me.'

Ralph nodded. 'I realise that now — though at the time, I was devastated.' He laughed self-consciously. 'I immediately bought my colours. I wanted to lose my life in some glorious battle on foreign soil!'

Emily smiled again. 'I'm glad you did not!'

'So am I, now!' His eyes twinkled

with happiness. 'I want to shout it to the world. She loves me! She loves me!' He beamed at her in wonderment of his good fortune.

Emily decided she wanted more than a beam of happiness. She leaned forward and tilted her face towards his. 'Will you kiss me?' she asked. 'Though it seemed impossible, I've dreamed and dreamed of it during the past few hours.'

'That is a dream you can hold for ever.' Ralph smiled as he lowered his head. 'I promise to kiss you every day of our lives!'

And he began to fulfil his promise.

Books by Karen Abbott
in the Linford Romance Library:

RED ROSE GIRL
SUMMER ISLAND
A TIME TO FORGIVE
LOVE IS BLIND
LOVE CONQUERS ALL
A MATTER OF TRUST
DESIGNS FOR LOVE
WHEN TRUE LOVE WINS
A TASTE OF HAPPINESS
THE HEART KNOWS NO BOUNDS
THE TURNING TIDE
OUTRAGEOUS DECEPTION
RISING TO THE CALL
A FRENCH MASQUERADE
A HEART DIVIDED
DANGER COMES CALLING
TO FACE THE PAST
DANGEROUS INTRIGUE
JUST A SUMMER ROMANCE
AN UNSUITABLE ALLIANCE
HER RELUCTANT HEART
AFRAID TO LOVE
TO CAPTURE A HEART

FAITH FOR THE FUTURE
A CHANGE OF HEART
ILLUSIONS OF LOVE
A DIVIDED INHERITANCE
ELUSIVE LOVE
THE FARRINGTON FORTUNE
A BRIDE FOR LORD MOUNTJOY
A LOVE WORTH WAITING FOR
THE NEW LORD WESTLAKE

Other titles in the
Linford Romance Library:

THE POWER AND THE PASSION

Joyce Johnson

After a failed business venture and a broken engagement, artist Abbie Richards takes advantage of an opportunity to do a year's English teaching in Sicily. There, she becomes involved with the large, extended Puzzi family; it's members wealthy and powerfully placed in the community. Abbie enjoys the teaching and the social life at Maria Puzzi's language school, and falls in love with charismatic surgeon Roberto Puzzi, only to find herself dangerously entangled in the Puzzi power struggles . . .

HOLD ME CLOSE

Margaret Mounsdon

Resting actress Sara Armitage is thrilled to be offered a job, even if it means looking after Lyle Jackson's young daughter Jenny. Sara and Lyle have history and when Carla de Courcy, now Lyle's ex-wife and Jenny's mother, appears back on the scene, Sara is forced to face up to her past. Will Lyle break her heart for a second time or is she strong enough to withstand her love for him?

LOVE ON ICE

Teresa Ashby

Dr Becky Hope's estranged husband is dying in a hospice, his mistress at his bedside. Distraught and exhausted, Becky turns to her colleague Dr Jake Lachlan, who at first is unaware that she's married. When he does find out, wanting to put some space between them, he joins an Antarctic expedition as a ship's medic — unaware that Becky is the second doctor. Although they try to avoid each other, dramatic events on board bring them unavoidably together . . .

THE GOLDEN CHALLENGE

Sheila Holroyd

As Civil War looms in England, Belinda tries to escape by fleeing to France with a fortune in gold. But there are others who want her treasure and trying to tell friend from foe makes life both difficult and dangerous. And should she please her father by marrying a man she does not love? For she is increasingly drawn to a man who wants her to abandon everything she knows to face the challenge of life in a new world . . .